Goddess Girls

APHRODITE
THE DIVA

I0383226

Goddess Girls

APHRODITE
THE DIVA

JOAN HOLUB & SUZANNE WILLIAMS

SCHOLASTIC INC.
New York Toronto London Auckland
Sydney Mexico City New Delhi Hong Kong

This book is a work of fiction. Any references to historical events, real people, or real locales are used fictitiously. Other names, characters, places, and incidents are the product of the authors' imagination, and any resemblance to actual events or locales or persons, living or dead, is entirely coincidental.

No part of this publication may be reproduced, stored in a retrieval system, or transmitted in any form or by any means, electronic, mechanical, photocopying, recording, or otherwise, without written permission of the publisher. For information regarding permission, write to Aladdin Paperbacks, an imprint of Simon & Schuster Children's Publishing Division, 1230 Avenue of the Americas, New York, NY 10020.

For Lucy and Alice Berliant

—J.H. and S.W.

CONTENTS

1   D FOR DIVA   *Page 1*

2   LONELY HEARTS CLUB   *Page 27*

3   THE LETTER   *Page 54*

4   ISIS   *Page 71*

5   MATCHMAKERS   *Page 98*

6   WORK, WORK, WORK   *Page 119*

7   GODBOYS AND PYRAMIDS   *Page 143*

8   PYGMALION'S CHOICE   *Page 166*

9   BOOM! ZAP! CRASH!   *Page 188*

10   HERA   *Page 215*

11   GALATEA   *Page 228*

12   GUESS WHO?   *Page 252*

1

D for Diva

I'M FAILING HERO-OLOGY? APHRODITE STOOD in the middle of the Mount Olympus Academy gymnasium and stared at her grade in shock. *That can't be!* she thought. She closed her sparkling blue eyes and opened them again, hoping she hadn't seen right. Unfortunately the D was still there. Okay, so a D wasn't exactly failing. But it was close.

She glanced around and saw mean-girl Medusa eyeing her in a nosy way from across the gym. *Uh-oh.* Quickly, she stuffed the reportscroll into the pocket of her new chiton. She'd work on somehow getting her grade changed later. But for now she'd better do what she'd come here for and get out fast before anyone asked about her grades. She couldn't let anyone find out about this. Plenty of students at MOA thought that anyone who was beautiful was automatically an airhead. She didn't want to reinforce the idea. Besides, it wasn't true!

Absently, she fluffed her long, naturally wavy golden hair. Sure, everyone said she was the prettiest goddessgirl at the Academy. But one bad grade didn't mean she was D for dumb. Right?

With her eyes glued to the giant game board which now hogged the center of the gym, Aphrodite hurried toward it. The board was normally set up in Mr. Cyclops's Hero-ology classroom. It had been moved here for a party to celebrate Hero Day. Today's party kicked off the start of Hero Week, a five-day school break.

"Excuse me. Sorry. Pardon me," she said, weaving through the throng of students between her and the game. Every godboy she saw was instantly dazzled by her smile and moved aside for her to pass. *Whew!* The gym was packed. Hero-ology was a required class, so every student at MOA had gathered here. She'd arrived late because she'd zipped down to the Immortal Marketplace bright and early for gift wrap and lost track of time. A window display had caught her eye and she'd wound up trying on one chiton after another. Could have happened to anyone, right?

Eventually, she reached the game board, which

covered the top of a table about the size of two Ping-Pong tables set side by side. Its three-dimensional world map showed colorful countries dotted with castles, villages, roads, and hills. The countries were surrounded by oceans filled with small sea monsters, mermaids, and scaly dragons that really moved!

Dozens of three-inch-tall hero statues stood atop the board here and there as movable game pieces. Most already had a small gift resting beside them. It was tradition that each student reward his or her hero on this special day. (Hence the need for her trip to the mall that morning for gift wrap!)

Unfortunately, the statue of Paris, her valiant mortal hero, had been set on the far side of the game board on Mount Ida in Asia. Aphrodite glanced back toward the gym door, wishing she could escape now.

But she couldn't leave without giving Paris the gift she'd brought for him.

Clutching her pink shopping bag, she began to pick her way around the edge of the huge game. Out of the corner of her eye, she saw one of her best friends, Athena. They waved to each other, wiggling their fingers. Athena's reportscroll was clasped to her chest and her face glowed with pride. Since she was the biggest brain in school, it was a no-brainer to guess that she'd made an A.

Hearing a *whoop*, Aphrodite looked over to see Apollo high-fiving with Artemis, another of her best friends. Obviously, the brother-sister twins were happy with *their* grades! Even Dionysus, who was a major goof-off, was proudly showing around his C. He'd done better than *she* had? No fair! Acting in school dramas and playing in Apollo's band were the only things he took seriously. Other than that, he pretty much joked around all the time. Well! She didn't think she deserved a D. And as soon as could, she was going to have a talk with Mr. Cyclops about changing her grade.

Aphrodite breathed a sigh of relief when she finally reached the far side of the game board. She dug into her shopping bag and took out a package wrapped in sparkly paper and tiny corkscrew ribbons. It was the gift she'd chosen to reward Paris.

"Here you go, little hero; I hope you like what I got you." As she spoke, the magical gift wrap began to unwrap itself. Inside the small gift box was a shiny gold shield about two inches tall. "It's one of a kind. Real fourteen-karat gold. I found it at the Immortal Marketplace and my godboy friend Hephaestus added the swirly monogrammed *P*. P for Paris. See?"

She set the shield on the game board next to him. Everything they did to their statues actually happened to the corresponding real mortal heroes living far below on earth. So that meant the life-size, living, breathing Paris had just received a big gold shield like this miniature one from her. And he could hear her voice, too, as if she was whispering in his ear.

"Sorry about making you fall in love with Helen," Aphrodite went on. "And about the problems it caused in Troy."

Their class assignment had been to send their heroes on quests. Instead, she'd accidentally helped Paris start a war. One teensy-weensy little mistake. Was that why she'd gotten a—*gulp*—D? Thinking about it made her remember that she was in a hurry to get out of there.

She maneuvered around the game board again, heading for the side door. Maybe she could slip out before anyone noticed how upset she was. Before anyone could ask her about—

A green hand fell on her arm. "Hey, how'd you do?" asked Medusa, stepping between her and the door to freedom. Aphrodite stopped dead, staring at the snakes that grew from Medusa's head in place of hair. They flicked their forked tongues in and out as they stared back at her with beady red eyes. Momentarily mesmerized by them, Aphrodite didn't say a word.

"Earth to Bubbles." Medusa snapped her fingers to get her attention.

Aphrodite's eyes flew to Medusa's face. "Stop calling me that." She hated the nickname. It was kind of embarrassing that she'd been born from sea foam, and *some* people never let her forget it.

"Oops. Sorry." Medusa shrugged, as if saying the nickname had only been an accident. "So did you get your grade?"

"Of course," Aphrodite replied casually. "How about you?"

"I got a B," Medusa said with a self-satisfied smirk.

Behind them, two godboys—Apollo and Ares—pushed their way up to the game board. Then they began noisily racing their heroes up and down the Mediterranean Sea in miniature ships. Several other students gathered to watch.

Medusa spoke more loudly to be heard over the commotion. "So what's your grade?"

Apollo glanced at Aphrodite over one shoulder. "Bet you got an A, like Athena."

"Yeah, Aphrodite's better at starting wars than anyone I know," added Ares. His eyes sparkled as he grinned over at her. Aphrodite couldn't tell if he'd meant that in admiration, or if he was teasing. As the godboy of war, he actually *might* think that starting a war was a good thing!

"I didn't do it on purpose!" she protested. "I just wanted Paris to find love."

"Yeah," growled Medusa, "only my hero, King Menelaus, was in love with her first."

Godsamighty! thought Aphrodite. *Get over it, already!* She jutted out her chin, blue eyes flashing. "Who's the goddessgirl of love around here anyway?" she demanded, setting a hand on her hip. "Me, that's who!" She thumped her chest for emphasis. "So I'm the one who should decide who falls in love!"

Medusa rolled her eyes. "You are *such* a diva!"

"Huh?" Aphrodite huffed, drawing back in surprise. What was she talking about?

"It's true!" Medusa insisted. "You'd do just about anything to get attention. Even start a war! But word is that the mortals on earth aren't exactly happy about that."

Aphrodite glared at her, something she wouldn't have dared do if she were a mortal. Medusa could turn mortals to stone with one stare. "I told you that was an accident."

"I think it's nice that she wanted to help Paris find love," Persephone interrupted, coming to stand beside Aphrodite.

"And as for the war—all of us have made mistakes with our heroes," said Athena, slipping between Aphrodite and Persephone and linking arms with both. "Just look how lost I got my Odysseus on his way home from Troy."

Persephone, Athena, Artemis, and Aphrodite were

all best friends, as well as the most popular goddess-girls at MOA. It was nice that her friends stuck up for her and their words gave Aphrodite a warm feeling. Still, what Medusa had said about the earthbound mortals' disappointment in her was troubling.

Before she could think more on that, though, Artemis spoke up from behind her. "Athena's right," she said. "The whole reason we're at MOA is to learn how to be the best goddesses we can be. Mistakes are part of the process. Besides, I thought the Trojan war made this year's Hero-ology class way more interesting than in past years."

"Yeah!" added Ares, glancing up from the game board race. "War's cool."

"That comment was *so* not helpful," Aphrodite informed him. She'd had an on-and-off crush on Ares all year long. No surprise. After all, he was tall, blond, and muscled—easily the cutest boy in school. But recently things had been even rockier between them than usual. So rocky that she was sure she was over him now. Very sure.

Medusa nudged her with an elbow. "So give it up. What was your grade?"

This girl was as irritating as a Harpy! It seemed to Aphrodite that half the class was listening by now. She didn't want to fib, but Medusa had forced her into it. Faking a bright smile, she said, "If you must know, I got a—"

CRASH! BOOM!

Everyone cringed and looked upward. The gym's domed roof was open to the sky, which was quickly filling with dark, angry clouds. A tremendous storm was blowing in, seemingly out of nowhere. Outside, hail the size of fists began to fall.

"Pull the roof!" Mr. Cyclops yelled. Ares, Apollo, and several other godboys rushed to begin tugging on the long ropes that operated the movable roof cover. Other students ducked under the bleachers to avoid the first raindrops that were falling in through the open roof.

Once the cover was in place, everyone, including Aphrodite, rushed to the windows and doors to peer outside. "Not again!" she heard someone mutter. It sounded like Athena.

Outside, Principal Zeus was stomping his way across the sports field. Since he was nearly seven feet tall with bulging muscles, a bushy red beard, and piercing blue eyes, he was a scary sight even on a normal day. In a bad mood, he was terrifying. And right now he seemed to be in a very, very bad mood, indeed!

His expression was fierce and his meaty hands were balled into fists. Wild storm winds whirled around him, whooshing scrolls out of passing students' hands, tangling their hair, and whipping at their chitons and togas. Thunderbolts crashed toward the ground, tearing up grass and splitting trees.

"Whoa," said Persephone. "Someone's grumpy today."

Aphrodite glanced at Athena. Aside from being King of the Gods, Ruler of the Heavens, and the principal of MOA, Zeus was also Athena's dad. Not surprisingly, her friend looked upset and a little embarrassed. It had to be hard for her to see him so angry. Aphrodite reached over and gave her hand a quick squeeze. Then she looked around for Mr. Cyclops. Apparently unfazed by the commotion outside, he was sitting alone at the table that held the Hero cake and other refreshments. Recognizing a chance to ask about her grade, and fueled with determination, she headed in his direction.

"Do you have a minute, Mr. Cyclops?" she asked sweetly. He'd been studying his grade book, and when he peered up at her, she jumped back in surprise. His humongous single eye appeared even more humongous than usual. He was wearing new glasses! Since he had only one eye in the middle of his forehead, there was only one lens, and it magnified his giant eyeball to twice its normal size.

He ducked his head as if he felt self-conscious about the new glasses, or rather, *glass*. "Nice specs . . . er . . . spec," she said, trying to put him at ease.

"Yes, well, my eyesight isn't what it used to be." He removed the glasses and laid them on his desk.

Thinking that it wouldn't hurt to buddy up to him

some more before asking about her grade, she added, "And that's a lovely pair of sandals you're wearing. Are they new too?"

His eye narrowed. "Is this about your grade?"

"Um . . ." she hedged. How had he guessed?

He held up a hand and shook his big, bald head. "Don't try to flatter me into giving you a better one. That kind of thing might work on godboys, but I'm immune."

She frowned at him, but quickly relaxed her expression again, remembering that frowns gave you wrinkles. "But I don't get it. I turned in all my assignments this year. I had perfect attendance."

"You turned in your assignments *late*. And half the time, you got to class late too. But that's not the reason for your low grade." He pointed toward the game board. "That is."

"You're still mad about what happened with Paris?"

"Mad?" Mr. Cyclops's single eyebrow rose. "You started a war among mortals on earth, Aphrodite. That's inexcusable. I've asked you numerous times to stop by my office to discuss your class work, yet you avoided me."

Aphrodite toyed with the GG charm—GG for Goddess Girl—that dangled from her golden necklace. Unfortunately, she knew that what Mr. Cyclops said was true. He *had* asked her to come by to chat earlier in the semester, but she'd been busy with her social life and hadn't gotten around to it. After all, what was more fun—shopping and hanging out with friends, or getting scolded by a teacher after school? Duh.

She darted a glance toward the other students. They were all still clustered around the windows and doors, peering out at Zeus. While their attention was on him, maybe she had enough time to make Mr. Cyclops see reason.

"Everyone makes mistakes," she said, repeating what her friends had said, and speaking softly so none of the other students would overhear. "Besides, war is such a strong word. I prefer to think of what happened in Troy as more of an . . . an unfortunate *incident.* I mean, you said you wanted us to test our heroes in ways that prove they're heroic. You said that otherwise they'd just be *ordinary* mortals. If I hadn't started the war—I mean the incident—the class wouldn't have been as challenging for the heroes or for the students. Right?"

Mr. Cyclops sighed. "Challenging your hero is one thing. A war is quite another. You're lucky Athena came up with the idea for the Trojan horse. If not for her, the war might *still* be going on. You should try to be more like her. Spend a little less time being a diva and more time on your studies."

"Diva?" Aphrodite flipped her long, lustrous golden hair over her shoulders, eyes sparkling with annoyance. Medusa had just called her the same thing. Obviously, they didn't know what they were talking about!

"Just try to remember that a goddess's actions affect everyone around her, mortal or immortal. Lots of folks on earth *and* at MOA are not too happy with you right now."

Another terrible crash drew their eyes to the entrance just in time to see one of Zeus's thunderbolts soar past. There was a loud crack as it struck a sundial in front of the gymnasium.

"See that?" squeaked Mr. Cyclops. "That's what I'm talking about!"

"You think it's *my* fault Principal Zeus is in a bad

mood?" Aphrodite turned her head from the door to look at her teacher, but his chair was empty now.

"I don't think. I *know*," said his shaky, muffled voice. It was coming from under the table! He must have only pretended to be unfazed. The last bolt had landed closer than the others and had finally unhinged him. Aphrodite lifted the edge of the white tablecloth and bent down to look at him. "Greek mortals are annoyed over your meddling," he went on, still cowering from the thunder. "Principal Zeus is getting flack from them. Which means I'm getting flack from him. We're all getting flack!"

Aphrodite wanted to ask what flack was. She figured it must be something icky since each mention of the word got Mr. Cyclops more and more worked up. But before she could ask, he went on.

"And when Zeus is in a bad mood, all the teachers

are in a bad mood. Which means YOUR GRADE
STANDS."

Aphrodite winced, hoping no one had heard him.
"What if I can figure out a way to convince mortals to
forgive me for starting the Trojan war—um, incident?"
she asked, beginning to feel desperate.

Mr. Cyclops crawled out from under the table and
sat in his chair again. Planting both elbows on the
tabletop, he gazed at her and tapped his fingertips
together as he did when something intrigued him. "A
community service project? Interesting idea. What
did you have in mind?"

Truth was, she didn't have anything in mind. She
wasn't even sure what he meant by "community service."
But she did know that mortals liked it when goddesses
did things for them. It made them feel special. Her

gaze skittered around the room, as she tried to think of something that would put a smile on Mr. Cyclops's face and a good grade on her reportscroll. Her eyes fell on Persephone and her crush, Hades. They were holding hands. Seeing them together like that reminded her of love, which reminded her that she was the goddessgirl of love (not that she ever *really* forgot). Why not use her matchmaking talent to help fix her grade? Thinking fast, she said, "I'll start a Lonely Hearts Club to help lonely mortals find love!"

"Hmm." Mr. Cyclops's eye blinked at her. "I don't know. Your matchmaking with Paris, Helen, and King Menelaus was a disaster. Why would this be any different?"

"Disaster is such a strong word," said Aphrodite. "I prefer to call it an unfortunate love triangle. Besides, how was I to know Medusa had already made King Menelaus fall in love with Helen too? Really, she's the one you should be mad at."

"If you'd been paying attention—"

"Nothing makes people happier than being in love," Aphrodite said quickly.

Mr. Cyclops studied her for a moment. Then he put on his glasses, and leaned toward her like he'd reached a decision. Aphrodite held her breath, hoping.

"All right. Forge ahead with your community service project," he told her. "If you give it your all, I'll raise you to a B. However, if you don't set things right with mortals by the end of the week, your D stands."

Her jaw dropped. "You want me to spend my vacation on this? But it's Hero Week! I was planning to go on a trip with my friends."

"Your choice," said Mr. Cyclops in a take-it-or-leave-it tone. "But I'd hate for you to have to repeat this semester of Hero-ology. And something needs to be done to get Zeus out of this funk." He gestured toward the uneasy students still gathered at the entrance. "Mortals and teachers aren't the only ones affected by his bad mood. Your classmates will eventually start looking around for a reason for it. And fair or not, you may get the blame."

Aphrodite heaved a huge sigh. Doing "community service" was not the way she'd planned to spend the holiday. But she didn't have much choice if she hoped to improve her grade, patch things up with mortals, and keep immortals from blaming her for Zeus's grumpiness. "Okay, I'll do it. And don't worry. The Paris-Helen thing was a fluke. I'm the goddessgirl of love, and nobody is better at matchmaking than I am. You'll see."

"Let's hope your enthusiasm translates into results," said Mr. Cyclops, in a voice that told her he wasn't truly convinced.

But she'd show him. As she left the gym and headed outside, her optimism was high. If she had to be stuck here during the break, at least she'd be doing what she loved best—matchmaking. Still, Hero Week was only five days long. She would need to do some fast advertising of her Lonely Hearts Club to get things rolling. Fortunately, she knew exactly who could help her with that.

Pheme, the goddessgirl of gossip.

2

Lonely Hearts Club

"PHEME! OVER HERE!" APHRODITE WAVED TO a goddessgirl with short, spiky orange hair as she reached the MOA courtyard outside. The storm had quieted, moving off into the distance after Zeus disappeared beyond the sports fields and the gymnasium. Aphrodite stepped around one of the thunderbolts he'd left behind, which was stuck point-down in one of the courtyard's marble tiles. The thunderbolt, which was as tall as she was, still sizzled and popped with electricity. As she hurried toward Pheme, she passed a custodian wearing thick gloves. He was pushing a wheelbarrow around the courtyard, plucking out smaller bolts that were stuck in the tiles, bushes, benches, and school walls. If Principal Zeus's bad mood continued much longer, MOA was going to fall apart!

"Guess what?" she told Pheme when she reached her. Then her news rushed out so fast, it almost sounded like one overly long sentence. "I'm starting a Lonely Hearts Club and it's going to be for mortals only. Mortals who are looking for love, that is. I want them to send me letters, then I'll find the perfect match for them. Think you could help me get the word out?"

Pheme's eyes lit with interest. "Definitely! Just let me be sure I got the facts straight. You're starting a

Lovely Hearts Club and you're inviting mortals who're in love to write you letters." Each word she spoke puffed from her lips like miniature smoke writing. Which, of course made it even easier for her gossip to spread, since it could not only be heard, but could also be seen floating in the air above her head!

"No! It's a *Lonely* Hearts Club," Aphrodite corrected her. "And it's for mortals who want to *find* love—wait, how about if I write it down for you?" She reached into her bag for her notescroll and her red feather quill pen.

But Pheme was already dashing off. "That's okay," she called back over her shoulder. "I've got it now, and I already see someone I can tell."

Aphrodite glanced at the group of goddessgirls Pheme seemed to be heading toward. "But the club's not for immortals!"

"I know, I know. Still, I have to be the first to spread the news around school about what you're doing during the break or I'll just die!"

"Be sure to go down to earth to let mortals know too!" Aphrodite called. "Tell them to send me their letters as soon as possible."

"Sure thing! I'll catch a ride in Hermes' delivery chariot in a few."

A little worried, Aphrodite watched as the girl paused halfway across the courtyard, veering off in a new direction to interrupt a conversation between two godboys. After she spoke to them, they both glanced toward Aphrodite. Then Pheme rushed over to two goddessgirls. After a moment, they too, looked over at Aphrodite and began to whisper. No doubt everyone was wondering why she was spending her holiday working. She'd have to think up a good excuse in case someone asked.

Pheme moved on again, jumping from group to group like a hopping flea. Aphrodite hoped she could be trusted to spread the news correctly. Sometimes the facts got twisted when Pheme was involved. Still, the girl had an amazingly wide social network and could spread news faster than a herald in a speeding chariot. And Aphrodite had no time to waste if she didn't want the whole school to think she was a D-making airhead.

Turning, she headed toward the olive grove that grew just beyond the courtyard. She was supposed to meet her friends there for a picnic to finalize their travel plans for the holiday. Now she was going to have to back out. She wasn't looking forward to giving them the bad news.

She found Athena and Persephone sitting on a picnic blanket surrounded by a ring of olive trees. Artemis lay on her stomach between them. Her three dogs were romping through the trees, chasing a magical bone-shaped ball that never stopped bouncing. There was a lunch basket on the edge of the blanket, and the girls were already munching ambrosia sandwiches and sipping nectar. Ambrosia and nectar were not only the food and drink of the gods—they also gave their skin a soft shimmery glow, which made them even more beautiful.

The center of the blanket was covered with a pile of scrolled vacation brochures and maps, and the girls were busy looking through them. "Hey! It's about time," said Athena, looking up. "Come help us decide where to spend the holiday."

Aphrodite joined them on the blanket and unrolled

one of the papyrus brochures. *Hmm.* There was a fashion show in Rome this week. Too bad she couldn't go.

Athena eagerly unrolled another brochure and laid it in the middle of the blanket for all to see. "I vote for this museum in Venice. Just look at all the pottery and urns!"

"Urns?" Artemis wrinkled her nose. "I've been learning stuff all semester. I want to have fun during break. Besides, museums don't allow dogs." Her bloodhound trotted over and she gave him a pat. His name was Suez—*Zeus* spelled backward.

"Well, what's *your* idea?" Athena asked.

Artemis quickly whipped four small rumpled pieces of papyrus from the pocket of her chiton. "Ta-da! Four tickets to the races at the Roman Colosseum. Only they're going to flood the track where the chariots normally race, and bring in real ships to race around in instead. Can you imagine?"

Persephone sighed. "We went to the Colosseum last year for Hero Week. How about something scenic this time instead?" She held up a brochure with pictures of flowers. "We could go to this flower show. See some tulips."

"Another flower show?" Athena said doubtfully. "I mean, flowers are pretty. But we already went to that one on earth a few months ago with your mom."

Persephone let the brochure drop to the blanket. "Okay, but we leave tomorrow. We have to agree on something!"

"We could try eeny, meeny, Minotaur, moe," suggested Artemis.

"No Minotaurs," said Persephone. "Someone might get hurt."

"Any ideas, Aphrodite?" asked Athena.

Aphrodite tossed the fashion brochure back onto the pile. "I'm sorry, but I can't go."

Her friends stared at her in dismay. "Why not?" asked Persephone.

"I've decided to stay at MOA," she said, trying to sound upbeat to hide her disappointment. "I'm planning to clean my room and do a little shopping. And you know, just relax."

Artemis sat up straight. "No way. Your room is already so clean I could eat off your floor."

"And you go shopping almost every weekend," said Athena.

"Yeah, what gives?" asked Persephone.

Aphrodite didn't want to lie to her friends any more than she had to, so she told them what she could. "The truth is—I'm staying here so I can start a Lonely Hearts Club. For mortals."

"Huh?" said Athena. "Why?"

Aphrodite stared at the three of them, stumped. She wasn't about to tell them the real reason for the club—that she'd made a D for dumb and was trying to bring up her grade with an extra-credit project. She didn't want her best friends to be embarrassed for her!

Persephone smiled uncertainly. "Mortals worship us all the time. I think it's nice that you want to do something for them."

"Sure. Great," Artemis added. "But not during the holiday!"

"Is it because you don't like our vacation choices?" asked Athena. She picked up a bunch of brochures and held them out to Aphrodite. "We'll let you pick. C'mon. Surely you don't want to spend this week here. My dad's cranky mood is making everyone miserable."

Artemis nodded. "Isn't that the truth? My last three archery practices were rained out."

"It's definitely been gloomy around here lately," Aphrodite agreed.

"Gloomy's okay sometimes," said Persephone. Hades lived in the Underworld and she sometimes visited him there. That place was definitely gloomy!

"Yeah, we're all getting tired of playing Dodge the Thunderbolts," said Artemis, abandoning the subject of where to vacation for the moment. She looked at Athena. "So what's up with your dad anyway? Do you know?"

Aphrodite froze, waiting to see if Athena would blame Zeus's bad mood on the war, um, incident she'd started in Hero-ology.

But Athena only looked down, toying with the ends of the shiny, braided gold belt at the waist of her chiton.

"Beats me," she said, shrugging. Then she looked at Aphrodite, her eyes wistful. "You *will* come on our trip, won't you? It won't be the same without you."

Aphrodite's heart sank. Athena looked so sad. It was reassuring that her friends would miss her if she stayed behind. Maybe she should go with them after all. Mortals were already disappointed in her. She didn't want to let her immortal friends down too!

BOOOM! Before she could reply, a tremendous crack of thunder sounded nearby, making them jump. "Uh-oh. Sounds like our unhappy principal is back from his walk," Artemis said as all three of her dogs yelped and tried to burrow under the blanket. They were terrified of thunder. "We'd better scram!" she added.

The thunder was a timely reminder of the likely reason for Zeus's bad mood, Aphrodite decided. Her mistake with Paris and Helen in Hero-ology. *I have to stick to my plan with the club and hope it satisfies Mr. Cyclops,* she reminded herself as she helped Athena and Persephone gather the brochures and blanket. There would be other vacations with her friends.

"Looks like this is going to be another bad one!" she said as Artemis grabbed the basket and tried to calm her three dogs. "I'm off to my room."

"Sure you won't change your mind? Why don't you come with us to the Immortal Marketplace to get some more travel brochures?" suggested Persephone.

Aphrodite hesitated, but then shook her head no. Looking at travel brochures might prove too tempting.

As rain began to fall, all four goddessgirls dug in their bags for their umbrellas, and popped them open. Aphrodite's was white with pink hearts and real diamonds; Artemis's was red with black dog silhouettes wearing sparkly ruby collars; Persephone's was decorated with glittering sapphire-centered flowers; and Athena's sported philosophical quotes and was edged with emeralds. Aphrodite had picked them all out and given them to the girls as gifts when Zeus's rainstorms had begun.

A quote by a famous Greek author named Plato on Athena's umbrella caught her eye: *At the touch of love everyone becomes a poet.* She smiled to herself. How true. "Stop by my room and tell me where you've decided to go before you head out, okay?" said Aphrodite.

"So you really won't go with us—to the marketplace *or* on vacation?" asked Athena as she, Persephone, and Artemis strapped on winged sandals.

Unexpectedly, tears welled up in Aphrodite's eyes. She shook her head, biting her lip to keep from crying.

At least her friends had stopped pressing her for the reasons she was staying put at MOA. "You'll have to count me out," she mumbled. "Have a good time though." With that, she made a dash through the rain for the school building. When she reached the courtyard, she glanced over her shoulder and saw her friends winging off in the opposite direction.

All over the courtyard, students were running for cover and opening umbrellas. Everyone at MOA carried one these days because you never knew when Zeus would kick up another sudden storm. Once inside the school, Aphrodite shook out her umbrella, then took the stairs up to her room on the fourth floor.

To cheer herself up, she got busy right away. At her desk, she pulled out her feather quill pen, a bottle of ink, and twenty sheets of letter-size pink papyrus. Deciding that might not be enough, she got out ten more sheets. Then she picked up a bottle of perfume and sprayed each sheet with a *poof* of fragrance. Ah! Eau de Goddess. It was her own personal fragrance, which Persephone had helped her concoct one semester in Beauty-ology class.

Any Lonely Hearts letters would arrive via one of the four magic winds—Aeolus, Boreas, Notus, and Zephyr. They were always whooshing around carrying mail to and from immortals. Usually, the winds just dropped letters through the windows at MOA. But now that she was expecting a huge pile of mail, she would need an actual mailbox. Otherwise, letters would wind up scattered all over her floor.

She dashed downstairs to the Craft-ology class-room on the second floor of the building and helped herself to the supply closet. Inside were shelves lined with scissors, tape, rulers, poster board, glitter, paint, clay, and boxes of every size and shape. She picked out a medium-size box, then decided it was too small for what she had in mind. She chose a larger one that stood as high as her waist. Setting it on a table, she got to work. An hour later, she finished decorating the box, and headed for the stairs again.

"What's that?" asked a curious voice.

Pausing three steps up, Aphrodite peeked around the box she held and saw Pandora, Athena's roommate, who'd been coming down the stairs toward her. As a symbol of her curiosity, Pandora's long blue-and-gold-streaked bangs took the shape of a question mark, plastered against her forehead.

"It's a mailbox," said Aphrodite. She turned the box to display the side she'd painted with swirly glittered letters that read: *Lonely Hearts Club*.

"You're starting a club?"

"Mmm-hmm." Aphrodite moved past her up the stairs. Pandora's questions never stopped. She would be here all day if she didn't escape now.

Unfortunately, Pandora only turned and followed her. "Who's it for? How many members do you have?"

Above her, Aphrodite was almost relieved to see Medusa, even if she was wearing her usual sour expression. Medusa's eyes moved over the box, reading the glittery sign. Aphrodite smiled at her, but Pandora reached for a pair of glasses with bright green lenses in her bag and put them on. All mortals had to hide their eyes from Medusa or risk being turned to stone. To solve the problem, which she had accidentally helped cause, Athena had invented "stoneglasses" for the mortals at MOA. Instead of protecting against the sun, they protected against being turned to stone by Medusa's stare.

"I'm starting a club to help mortals find love," Aphrodite told the two girls.

"Oh, really? Why?" said Medusa, folding her arms and looking skeptical.

"For fun," Aphrodite said quickly. Only a few mortals attended MOA, and Pandora and Medusa were among them. She hoped they wouldn't want to join her club. Even she couldn't be that unlucky! Before they could question her further, she rushed past them to her room.

Her eyes widened when she saw five letterscrolls lying on the floor just below her window. Wow! If mortals were this eager for her help, maybe they weren't as mad as Mr. Cyclops assumed, Aphrodite thought with excitement. This whole community-service thing was going to be a snap.

After picking them up, she positioned the new

mailbox under her window. Then she sat on her bed and opened the letters with her silver letter opener, unrolling them one by one. She was disappointed to see that the first three were from godboys who were crushing on her. That was nothing new. Godboys were always vying for her attention. Each of them had written that they admired her beauty, but none of them said they admired her brains or anything else about her. Did they think she was *all* beauty and nothing more? Well, if they did, they were wrong, and she was going to prove it!

The fourth letter turned out to be even worse. A mortal bear-giant on earth named Agrios wanted to join her club. He had written that he was interested in meeting lots of sweet maidens, especially those who had good taste. *Humpf!* Did he really think she was too dumb to read between the lines? Everyone knew that bear-giants ate mortal maidens. She tossed that one into the trash. She was trying to help members of her club find love, not dinner!

She opened the fifth letter, hoping this one would be a genuine plea for help. Instead, it turned out to be a riddle!

YOU'VE GOT THE SMARTS
TO HELP LONELY HEARTS.
GOOD LUCK WITH YOUR NEW CLUB.
~ FROM GUESS WHO LIKES YOU?

How nice! At least someone out there thought she had some brains. Under her fingertips, she could feel magic fizzing within the papyrus. That meant that the riddler was most likely an immortal. She fanned the letter, wondering who it could be from. Hephaestus maybe? He had once told her she was clever. She certainly hoped he wasn't falling in like with her again, as he had earlier in the year. He was nice. She didn't want to hurt him by rejecting him a second time. Just a few days ago, she'd seen him walking hand in hand with a goddessgirl named Aglaia that Aphrodite herself had introduced him to. The two of them had looked so happy together. Had they broken up?

Going to the window, she checked the sundial outside. It was noon. Pheme was probably down on earth spreading the news about her club right this very minute. As she straightened her already-neat room and fluffed up her heart-shaped pillows, she imagined the excitement her news must be causing. Mortals would be lining up for her help. Everyone wanted to find love, right?

But as the hours passed, no more letters arrived.

Aphrodite did her nails, cleaned her closet, and read the latest news in *Teen Scrollazine*. It was full of articles like: *The Hottest Godboys* (Naturally, Hades was tops on that list!) and *Five Fixes for a Bad Hair Day* (This article included a drawing of Medusa). There was also a quiz called: *What Godboys Really Want.* That got her thinking. She should create her own quiz to send each of her club members—as soon as she got any, that is. The information they provided on the quiz would help her help them to find love more efficiently. She sat at her desk and got to work on it.

It took her a couple of hours to finish and to make ten copies of it, but during that whole time no more letters came. She was beginning to wonder if mortals might be more annoyed with her than she'd realized—so annoyed that they didn't trust her to help them anymore! Or maybe Pheme just hadn't gotten the word out properly. Perhaps she'd better go check things out.

She stepped to the window. Letting her dark, curly eyelashes flutter closed, she concentrated on bringing an image of her favorite bird to mind. As she held on to that image, her body became lighter and smaller. She began to sprout soft emerald-colored feathers and her arms became wings. Soon she had shape-shifted into a lovebird! Flapping her delicate wings, she rose into the air and sailed from her window. Free as a bird now, she rode the wind from MOA, down through the clouds toward earth.

There she spotted a group of Greek mortals, who were laughing uproariously. Wondering what the joke was, she swooped lower to eavesdrop, coming to rest on a tall cypress tree just above them.

"Have you heard the news?" one mortal youth asked

another. "Aphrodite is starting a Lonely Darts Club. I guess it's for lonely mortals who like to play darts."

Oh no! thought Aphrodite. Pheme must have garbled the message she'd sent. No wonder no one had sent her any letters! Who would join a club like that?

"No! *I* heard it was a Bonely Smarts Club for mortals with intelligent dogs," insisted another mortal youth.

"You're both wrong!" said a maiden. "I heard it's a Foamy Arts Club for those who like to create bubble art while taking a bath."

"Who cares?" said the first mortal youth. "They're all the dumbest ideas I've ever heard!" They burst out laughing again.

Aphrodite's little bird cheeks went pink with embarrassment. How could she have trusted Pheme not to mess up? As more mortals joined the first three, the jokes about her club were told again and again. The sound of their laughter cut through her like an arrow. But then her feelings of hurt turned to anger. How dare these mortals make fun of her? She was a goddess! Didn't they know they risked her revenge? She'd be within her rights to turn them into mice, or beetles, or even toadstools! But if she did, she doubted it would make them want to join her Lonely Hearts Club. Instead, it would only make them madder. She'd look worse in their eyes than she already did, and the jokes about her club would likely spread even faster. Nope. Not worth it.

As she winged her way back to MOA, her heart felt so heavy it was a wonder she could fly at all. If word ever reached mortals that she'd made a D in a class, they'd be convinced she was too dumb to be worshipped. And there was a tiny part of her that wondered if they were right. Then she remembered the riddle-letter she'd gotten a few hours ago and felt somewhat comforted. At least there was one person at MOA besides her best friends who thought she was smart, even if she wasn't sure who it was.

She flew higher and higher until finally she broke through the clouds. Up ahead, MOA came into view, gleaming in the sunlight atop the highest mountain in Greece. It was an awesome sight that never failed to amaze her. Five stories tall and built of white marble, it was surrounded on all sides by dozens of Ionic columns and low-relief friezes. It was hard not to smile at such a glorious vista, and she felt both sides of her beak curve upward.

When she landed on her windowsill, Aphrodite poked her feathered head in her mailbox. A new letter had come! She pecked at it and didn't feel any magic in it. Which meant it was from a mortal. At last! A mortal looking for true love . . . she hoped.

3
The Letter

APHRODITE SHAPE-SHIFTED BACK INTO HER
goddessgirl form, hopped from the window ledge into
her room, and then pulled the letterscroll from her
mailbox. Unrolling it, she quickly discovered that it
was only *part* of a letter. Somehow, it had gotten torn
on its journey from earth to her and the last half of
many of the words had been ripped away. How disap-

pointing! She searched the mailbox, but it was empty. Where was the missing half?

The letter was addressed to:

Lon

Hea

Clu

The missing letters were easy to guess:

Lonely

Hearts

Club

At least the message about her club had reached *someone* correctly! But with so much of it missing, she wondered how this letter had even found her.

The writing inside proved impossible to decipher. She would need someone supersmart to help her figure it out. Throwing open her door, she rushed down the hall to Athena's room. But there was no answer when she knocked. Had her friends left for their trip while she was gone? No, they surely would've left a message for her since they'd promised to come by before leaving.

She rushed back down the hall to tap on the door to Artemis's room, which was next to her own. She'd never been so happy to hear Artemis's dogs bark in response. It meant her friends hadn't left yet after all. Sure enough, the door opened and Artemis said, "Hey, come on in. I'm packing."

Aphrodite eyed the messy room. There were bags of dog food and treats, dog toys, dog blankets, and books about dogs all over the floor. All three dogs were staring at her from the bed they shared, opposite Artemis's unmade one.

"I was worried you'd already left!" Aphrodite exclaimed in relief. "Where's Athena?"

"Probably in the cafeteria with Persephone. I was just about to go down there too. We couldn't decide where to go on our trip, so we're going to have dinner and then toss a coin. We'll head out for wherever tomorrow morning."

"I haven't eaten either," said Aphrodite. "Want to go together? Now?"

Artemis looked surprised at her hurry, but then shrugged good-naturedly. "Sure." She looked at her dogs. "Enjoy your naps, guys." They yawned and closed their eyes as she shut the door behind her.

The two goddessgirls headed for the cafeteria. It was only half as full as normal, since many students had already left on holiday. Athena and Persephone were sitting at the girls' usual table.

"What's that?" Athena asked the minute she saw the torn scroll in Aphrodite's hand.

Aphrodite held it up. "A letter from a Lonely Heart. Well, half a letter."

"Maybe it's from a broken heart," Artemis joked.

"I'm pretty sure it's from a mortal writing to me for help. See?" Aphrodite unrolled the letter on the table for her friends to see. Pointing to the "Lon Hea Clu," she said, "I'm sure this part says 'Lonely Hearts Club.'"

"Hmm," said Persephone. "The magic wind must have gotten 'wind' of your club and puzzled that part out in order to deliver it to you."

Aphrodite nodded. "I was hoping you all could help me figure out what the rest of it says."

Athena studied the letter, her interest caught. "I love puzzles."

"Me too," said Persephone.

"Ditto," added Artemis.

Athena picked up the letter and read it aloud:

Dᴇᴀʀ Gᴏᴅᴅᴇꜱ

I ᴀᴍ ᴀɴ ᴀᴍᴀᴢ

ʙᴜᴛ ᴏɴʟʏ ᴀ ᴍᴏ

I ᴡᴀɴᴛ ᴛᴏ ꜰɪɴᴅ ʟ

Pʟᴇᴀꜱᴇ ʜᴇʟᴘ ᴍ

Sɪɢɴᴇᴅ,

Sᴀᴅ ʙᴏʏ ɪɴ G

Yᴏᴜ

Pʏɢ

"'*You Pig*'? He's calling you a pig?" Artemis jumped up and grabbed the bow and quiver of arrows she always had at the ready. "Nobody calls a goddess a pig and gets away with it," she growled. "I'll hunt him down and make him apologize!"

"Calm down," said Athena, giggling. "I think the whole letter probably said: 'Yours truly, Pyg.'"

Artemis wrinkled her nose, plopping back down in her chair. "Still—he doesn't sound promising for your club," she told Aphrodite. "What girl wants a pig for her crush?"

"Just because his name is Pig doesn't mean he *is* a pig," said Persephone. "Besides, it's probably only the beginning of a longer name. Like Pignificent or Pigmeister or something."

"Oh, *much* better," said Artemis, laughing.

"It's Pyg with a *y*, not an *i*," said Aphrodite. "And I believe there's a crush for everyone, no matter what they look like or what their name is or how rich or poor they are. Still, I can't match this boy with the right girl if I can't find him. Can anyone decipher more of the letter?" she asked.

Athena scrunched up her face, thinking. "As best I can tell, he's looking for something that starts with an *l*, and is hoping for help in finding it."

"*L* for love," said Aphrodite. "That part's easy, anyway."

"What are those squiggles and lines at the bottom? A map?" asked Persephone.

Athena nodded. "Probably showing his location." She glanced at Aphrodite. "I'm afraid you'll never find him with only half a map. And there's no return address."

"Where could *C* be?" mused Persephone.

"I know—China!" guessed Artemis.

"It could be any of a hundred places," said Athena, shaking her head.

Suddenly, there was a loud banging outside the cafeteria window, as small bits of hail hit the glass. Everyone in the cafeteria turned to look.

"Zeus?" Persephone wondered aloud.

"I don't think so," said Athena. "His storms are wilder." The student nearest to the window opened it.

WHOOSH! A magic wind blew inside and rushed here and there, ripping messages from the school bulletin board on the cafeteria wall. Then it headed straight for their table, blowing napkins onto the floor in its wake.

The wind whooshed around Aphrodite three times. "Godness!" she shouted, putting both hands on top of her head. "Stop it! You're messing up my hair!" But when the wind lifted the half-letter from the table, she grabbed it and held it to her chest. "What do you think you're doing? This letter's mine!"

The magic wind replied in rhyme, as usual:

I must take it away.

Where to, I can't say.

"Why not?" Aphrodite demanded.

The wind sighed.

I must speak in rhymes

and as far as I know,

there's nothing that rhymes

with the place it must go.

"Give us a hint," suggested Athena. "See if we can guess."

As if needing a minute to think, the mischievous wind whipped around the room, lifting togas and chitons, causing godboys and goddessgirls to shriek and hold down the hems of their clothing. Then it whooshed back to their table and announced:

To a faraway land

with pyramids and sand.

"Egypt?" guessed Aphrodite.

That is righty, Aphrodite! the wind murmured.

She groaned. Sometimes a magic wind's rhymes could get tiresome.

"But why take Aphrodite's letter to Egypt?" Persephone asked.

The wind replied:

Isis commands it.

Isis demands it.

The four goddessgirls leaned their heads together over the table. "Who's Isis?" Artemis whispered. But no one knew.

"I'll take it to Isis for you," Aphrodite told the wind.

When it replied, the wind sounded uncertain:

Highly irregular!

Not sure what to do!

It paused, then added:

Can you promise me

your word is true?

"Of course!" said Aphrodite. "Just tell me where—"
But the wind had already whooshed back out through
the window, before she could ask for a more specific
address.

Aphrodite looked at the others. "How am I supposed
to keep my word when I don't even know who or
exactly where this Isis person is?"

Persephone raised and lowered her shoulders.
"Egypt is a big place." It was, of course, what everyone
else had been thinking.

"Let's get some dinner," Artemis told Aphrodite.
"We'll think better on full stomachs."

By the time they returned with their trays, Athena
and Persephone had figured out something more. "We
think the *C* in the letterscroll might stand for 'Cairo,'"
said Athena. "That's the capital of Egypt. Maybe you'll
find Isis and the boy who wrote the letter there."

"Smart thinking!" said Aphrodite, opening her carton of nectar. Then a brilliant idea struck her. Looking around the table, she grinned at her friends. "Anyone up for a trip to Egypt?"

Athena's face lit up. "I've always wanted to see the pyramids. And that means we could all be together."

"Yeah. You know, there's a flower in Egyptian paintings called the lotus. I'd love to see a real one," said Persephone, sounding intrigued.

"What would I do there?" asked Artemis, munching her ambrosia burger.

"I believe the Egyptians are animal-lovers," Athena told her. "Would that interest you? I've heard they consider their pets almost like family!"

"Really?" Artemis brightened. "Okay, I'm in."

"Thanks, you guys!" said Aphrodite, feeling happiness bubble up in her for the first time since she'd found out her grade that morning.

"How will we travel?" asked Persephone.

"We can't take my chariot," said Artemis. "Going to Greece is one thing. But to get to Egypt, we'll have to cross the Mediterranean Sea. My deer couldn't make such a long trip."

"How about my swan cart?" said Aphrodite. "I haven't used it for a while, but it should still work. And it's great for long-distance travel."

"It's smaller than my chariot though," Artemis said doubtfully. "Will my dogs fit?"

"No, and even if they did, my swans are scared of them. Do you mind leaving them behind for a few days?" Aphrodite crossed her fingers under the table. She liked Artemis's dogs, but they would be trouble on a long trip.

Artemis shook her head. "I can't just leave them

alone here. They're my buddies. Who would take care of them?"

"I bet Hades would let them hang out with his dog," said Persephone.

"They'd love Cerberus. And the Underworld," Athena encouraged. "There are lots of places to romp and plenty of weird smells. A dog paradise."

"But will Hades be okay with watching them?" asked Artemis.

"He and some other godboys who are sticking around MOA during the holiday were going to try out Poseidon's new surf pool later. After you finish eating, we can go ask him."

"I'm going to hit the library before it closes," Athena told them, standing up. "I want to study up on hieroglyphics before we leave." She looked happier than Aphrodite had seen her in quite a while. "I'm so glad we're all going to be together. And I really need to get away from MOA for a while."

Watching her go, Aphrodite said, "I think Athena's more upset about her dad's mood than she lets on."

Persephone nodded, looking concerned. "Should we ask her about it?"

Aphrodite shook her head. "When she's ready to talk, she will. Until then, let's just be there for her." She stood and gathered her tray, and Artemis and Persephone did the same.

"Assuming Hades agrees to watch my dogs, let's meet in the courtyard tomorrow morning, okay?" suggested Artemis. "Then we can leave from there."

"Sounds good," said Aphrodite. After tossing her trash, she went to her room to pack. She was excited about going on holiday with her friends after all, but hoped it wouldn't turn out to be a wild-goose chase.

She had only five days of vacation and couldn't afford to waste one. What if the *C* in the letterscroll actually stood for something beside Cairo? Maybe it was the name of a store or restaurant, like the *Caledonian Pizza Kitchen* or *Cleo's Cosmetics* or *Calypso's Closets*.

Ooh, speaking of closets, she needed to pack her stuff. She threw open both of her closets, gazing upon the dozens and dozens of stunning chitons she owned. She tapped a pink-tipped fingernail on her chin, thinking. Forget what the *C* in the letterscroll stands for—the more important question was—what did one wear to an exotic land like Egypt?

4

Isis

WHEN SHE WOKE THE NEXT MORNING, Aphrodite found two more letterscrolls had arrived, but not through the window. These had been flattened and pushed under her door from the hallway. Had some godboys sneaked into the girls' hall with them? She'd been up late packing and was in no mood for any more compliments on her beauty. But when she unrolled the letters, she saw it was even worse than she'd expected. They were from Medusa and Pandora!

She plopped down on her bed, and read them with increasing dismay. Both girls were looking for love. She'd wanted mortals to write her for help, but not these two! Still, they *were* mortal, so they qualified for her Lonely Hearts Club. But finding the right guys for a mean, green girl with snaky hair, and a girl who did nothing but ask questions would not be easy.

Also, Medusa and Pandora hung out with immortals at school. So which would they prefer—mortal boys or immortal? Maybe even they didn't know. And sometimes people thought they wanted one thing, but another really suited them better. Still, if she asked the right questions, maybe, just maybe, she could find matches for them.

Remembering the quizzes she'd prepared, she grabbed two of them and wrote a note at the top of each to return the quizzes once they'd been filled out. Still in her nightgown, she left her room and zipped down the hall, slipping the quizzes under the two girls' doors. As for their answers, she was hoping for the best, but expecting the worst. At least it would give her a chance to test out her quiz.

Mortals and immortals alike could be so dim when it came to love, she thought as she got dressed, styled her hair, and put on her makeup. They often didn't notice when someone was interested in them. Or sometimes they crushed on someone who was entirely unsuitable. She enjoyed guiding them in the right direction, helping them to fall in love—or at least in like—with someone who might actually make them happy.

It was like a sixth sense, this ability she had to note every intrigued glance, every flicker of interest in a person's eye. Without even trying, she was always aware of who liked whom and usually guessed when a romance was budding well before those involved did.

But she'd never noticed any boy—mortal or immortal—showing an interest in Medusa or Pandora. If she *could* find the perfect crushes for them, she'd deserve to be crowned as the *queen* goddessgirl of love!

After she was dressed, Aphrodite stood before her full-length mirror and gave herself a critical once-over. Her Rubylicious-Red nail polish and the silk ribbons she had threaded through her long, wavy golden hair matched her red chiton perfectly. Her sandals and heart-shaped earrings matched them as well. As always, she wore her gold Goddess Girl necklace with its GG charm. But she needed another hint of gold to balance it out, she decided. Slipping a fat gold bracelet on her left wrist, she pronounced herself ready to meet this Isis girl, whoever she was.

Just before she left her room, she went to her knickknack shelf and reached for the small ceramic double-swan cart. Its two swans sat side by side, pulling a golden cart behind them. Although it was intricately designed, the figurine was so small, it fit in her hand. The swans' faces were turned toward each other. With their orange beaks pressed together and their necks gracefully curved, they formed the shape of a perfect heart between them.

Aphrodite had mysteriously received the cart when she was a baby, so it was dear to her. She liked to think that her mom, whoever she was, had left it with her to keep her safe and as a message to say that she'd loved her. Slipping the swan cart inside her handbag, she headed off to meet her friends.

Just outside the school's bronze doors, she met Mr. Cyclops on the stairs that led down to the courtyard. Her eyebrows rose at the sight of him. He was wearing plaid shorts, black socks, brown sandals, and a shirt decorated with palm trees. Well, it was his vacation too, she supposed. Still, it was weird seeing a teacher in normal—well, sort of normal—everyday clothes outside of class.

He noticed her travel case, and his unibrow rose too. He was probably wondering if she was going on a trip instead of doing the work she'd promised. "How's your extra-credit project going?" he asked.

"Fine," she said, trying to sound positive. "Medusa and Pandora joined my new club this very morning." Of course, so far they were her only club members, but she didn't mention that.

Mr. Cyclops scratched his bald head. "I'm afraid they don't count. After all, they're your friends."

Medusa—a friend? Is he for real? Aphrodite wondered. They did *not* get along. In fact, she halfway wondered if Medusa was trying to trick her somehow by asking to join her club.

"Well, you'll be pleased to know that I'm on my way to Egypt to investigate a mysterious letter I got from a mortal boy who's looking for love," she told him.

"Excellent!" he told her. "I'm glad you're taking your project so seriously."

"Oh, I am," she told him sincerely. Then she trotted down the rest of the steps.

When she reached the courtyard, she pulled the little swan cart from her handbag. Setting it in one palm, she stroked a fingertip over each swan's snowy white back. Then she gently placed it at the bottom of the stairs and stepped back, chanting:

"Feathered swans, wild at heart.

Spread your wings to fly my cart!"

She smiled to herself, reminded of the magic wind. Seemed like most things that involved magic often involved rhyme as well. As her words died away, the two swans fluttered, shaking their heads as if awakening from a deep sleep. Then slowly they began to unfurl their wings, growing ever larger in size. By the time their wings were fully spread, the swans were ten feet tall with wingspans of twenty feet! She petted their long, curved throats.

"Ready?"

Aphrodite looked up to see her three goddessgirl friends coming down the stairs to meet her. The small golden cart had grown along with the swans and was encrusted with splendid jewels that sparkled in the morning light. It was now big enough for six to sit comfortably. Or for four goddessgirls and their travel cases.

Persephone and Athena each tossed one case into the cart and climbed aboard.

Thonk! Aphrodite stashed hers as well.

Persephone's eyes widened. "Godness! What's in that thing?"

"Necessities," said Aphrodite. "Makeup, hair gel, perfume, lip gloss, a dozen chitons, jewels." She looked at Artemis. "Where's your case?"

"Here," said Artemis. She tossed a small knapsack into the cart.

"That's it?" asked Aphrodite, astonished.

"Including today, we'll be gone five days or less. So I brought four chitons. All I need." She hopped into the cart and Aphrodite joined her. Artemis's chitons had to be wrinkled in that bag, but somehow she always looked nice in spite of her inattention to clothing. Besides, Aphrodite could always lend her something to wear if she needed it.

Once their luggage was stowed, and the girls were securely seated, Aphrodite called out: *"To Egypt! Up and Away!"* Immediately the swans' enormous, brilliant white wings began to flap and they rose gracefully from the courtyard, pulling the golden cart behind them.

The swans glided smoothly away from Mount Olympus, their long necks stretched almost straight ahead of them as they sailed southeastward over Greece. Soon the girls saw nothing but blue below them as they crossed high above the Aegean and Mediterranean Seas. Here and there the water was dotted with islands covered with lush green plants and small houses painted in bright colors of red, turquoise, and peach. A mortal girl and boy ran out of one of the houses to wave excitedly at them and the goddessgirls waved back.

An hour later, the northern shore of Africa appeared ahead of them, separated by a wide river that branched off from the sea.

"It's the Nile!" called Athena. They followed the Nile River southward, toward the city of Cairo. A flock of seagulls flew alongside them for a while, then veered back toward the beach as their cart moved inland. Now desert stretched out in all directions below them instead of sea. Mortals dressed in long white robes and wearing fat turbans atop their heads rode camels across the sand.

Persephone elbowed Athena and pointed west

toward a trio of giant monuments, each with four triangular sides. "Pyramids! The biggest one is called the Great Pyramid of Giza. It's where kings were buried."

"Is that supposed to be a lion?" asked Artemis, staring at an enormous statue between them and the three pyramids.

"It's the Great Sphinx," said Athena. "It has the body of lion, but its head is that of a king."

They flew on until they reached the outskirts of Cairo. Then Aphrodite called to the swans in a voice as soft as a gentle breeze:

"Feathered swans, wild at heart.

Take us low and land our cart."

As soon as they touched down and stepped onto the street, both swans and the cart immediately shrank into a figurine again. Aphrodite tucked it into her handbag. Then they set their three travel cases and knapsack under a tree and chanted a magic spell that made them invisible to mortal eyes. The mosaic-tiled street led them into Cairo and they soon found themselves in the middle of a bustling bazaar.

Dozens of spice shops lined the street, selling baskets full of seeds, flowers, and herbs such as dried rosemary, sage, oregano, and wild basil. There were cut-glass bottles containing perfumes. There were bins of powdered spices including bright red chili powder and yellow saffron. There were pistachio nuts, tea, honey, eucalyptus, dried fruits, and cloves. One shop sold woven baskets in geometric designs and brightly patterned silk scarves stacked high on wooden tables.

"Ooh! Shopping!" said Aphrodite, her blue eyes sparkling at the sight of it all.

Artemis groaned. "I didn't come all this way to

shop. Don't you have a mortal named Pyg to find? And some girl named Isis?" But then she heard a squawk and noticed a pet boutique with iguanas, peacocks, and parrots. "Oh, well, maybe that can wait," she said, striking out for the shop.

"Just a sec," said Athena. She held out her hand. In her palm were four identical rings with unusual markings on them. "Put these on. They're translation rings. I asked Hephaestus to make them for us last night. They'll decode Arabic languages, so we'll understand the Egyptians when they speak, and they'll understand us."

"Good thinking," said Persephone. They each slipped a ring on and set out to shop. Aphrodite quickly lost herself among the makeup and clothing stalls, and soon held a bag of kohl, scarab jewelry carved from alabaster, and silks. Persephone approached one of the spice merchants and began testing fragrances, which she discussed animatedly with the shopkeeper. And Athena became absorbed in racks of rolled-up papyrus maps and travelscrolls.

Suddenly *ooh*s and *ah*s rippled through the crowded bazaar. Aphrodite and her friends turned to see four exotic Egyptian girls headed their way. All wore long linen dresses, had dark hair, and were stunningly beautiful in distinctly different ways.

One had her hair in a high silky ponytail and wore a bright blue dress. It was impossible to know the color of her eyes, for she was looking down at a textscroll, reading as she walked.

Another wore a long black linen dress with a necklace of black feathers. Her straight hair reached down to her hips, and atop her head, was a strange cone-shaped hat made of wax.

A third girl wore her hair in dozens of thin braids, each with a golden bead at the end. Her gown was yellow, and a matching yellow-and-white-striped cat slept curled around the back of her neck, almost as if it were a fashion accessory.

But most glamorous of all was the girl in the lead. She wore a long, violet-colored linen gown with a wide collar made of jeweled beads. Gold bracelets circled her wrists, rings adorned her fingers, swirly gold bands rode high on her arms, and golden pyramid earrings dangled from her ears. Her shiny, smooth black hair was thick, straight, and strung with emeralds and amethyst beads. It swayed back and forth like flowing silk as she strolled through the bazaar.

The girl's makeup was flawless too, Aphrodite couldn't help noticing. Her light green eyes were lined with kohl in a way that made her look fascinating and mysterious. Aphrodite knew her own blue eyes were beautiful, but light green eyes were both beautiful and *rare*. Jealousy sprang up in her, as green as the other girl's eyes.

Persephone nudged her. "Aphrodite?"

"Huh?" Aphrodite straightened, realizing she had been staring. But the girl with green eyes had been staring back.

Artemis leaned toward a nearby shopkeeper and Aphrodite heard her whisper, "Who's that in the purple?"

He smiled. "That's Isis, the goddess of love."

Aphrodite's jaw dropped. She heard her three friends gasp and felt them step closer, as if rallying around to protect her.

"Who does that Isis think she is?" Athena murmured.

"The goddess of love, indeed," said Persephone.

"She can't get away with that!" said Artemis.

Aphrodite nodded. "There's room for only one goddess of love in the world, and that's me." Sure, Isis was exotic and mysterious. But, hey! What kind of lovegoddess didn't wear even a hint of pink or red? Those were the true colors of the heart!

Isis stepped forward. "You're visitors to our land, yes? Welcome. I'm Isis, and these are my friends: First, Hathor," she said, pointing to the girl in blue, who glanced up from her textscroll, seeming only then to notice them. "Also, Ma'at." The girl wearing feathers and black dipped her chin. "And Bastet." The girl with the cat gave them a small smile.

Aphrodite introduced herself and the others in return. "We're goddesses too," she said.

Isis looked surprised. "Really? What kind?"

"The true kind," Artemis said pointedly.

"From Mount Olympus," added Athena.

"Where?" asked Hathor, looking confused.

"You mean you've never heard of it?" asked Persephone in surprise. The Egyptian girls shook their heads. Isis's beads clicked as her silky hair swung back and forth.

"Well, we've never heard of you either," Aphrodite said snootily, folding her arms.

Now it was the Egyptian goddesses' turn to gasp. Suddenly, Aphrodite and Isis were nose to nose, headed for a fierce argument.

Before either could say a word, Artemis asked, "Hey! Isn't that the other half of your letter?"

Aphrodite looked down to see that Isis did indeed have half of a letter stuck in her belt. "I think you have something that belongs to me," she told the Egyptian goddess, reaching for it.

"It's addressed to the goddessgirl of love," said Isis, twitching away.

"Right. And that's me," said Aphrodite.

Isis laughed. "I don't think so."

"Then why did I get the other half?" Aphrodite pulled her part of the letter from her bag and showed it to Isis. Hathor let out a snarky little snort, and Isis shot a worried look at her, as if she didn't quite trust her.

Aphrodite raised her brow. "Let's hold both halves up and see what it says," she suggested.

"Then what?" asked Isis, sounding suspicious.

"If the letter gives directions to Pyg's house, I'm going to see him is what."

"Who's Pig?" Ma'at asked in surprise. Hathor and Bastet shrugged as if to say they had no idea. Of course, his name was on Aphrodite's half of the letter, not Isis's.

"If you go, you take me with you," said Isis. "Or you can forget about seeing my half."

"All right," Aphrodite agreed. What choice did she have?

"Pinky swear," Isis insisted.

In answer, Aphrodite stuck out her little finger. Isis hooked hers around it and they briefly locked pinkies. Pinky swear was obviously a universal language. Then they laid both halves of the letter side by side on the nearest shop counter. As the other goddessgirls crowded around, Aphrodite and Isis read it aloud:

DEAR GODDESS OF LOVE,

I AM AN AMAZING SCULPTOR,
BUT ONLY A MORTAL BOY.
I WANT TO FIND LOVE.

PLEASE HELP ME.

SIGNED,

SAD BOY IN CYPRUS.

YOURS TRULY,

PYGMALION

"So Pyg's full name is Pygmalion," said Artemis, pronouncing it "Pig-MAY-lee-yuhn."

"And the *C* is for the island of Cyprus," said Persephone.

"Where's that?" asked Aphrodite.

"Near Turkey, east of Greece and north of Egypt," said Athena. "Remember the game board in Hero-ology?"

Aphrodite shut her eyes, envisioning the game board. She hadn't paid that much attention to where the countries were, but now she wished she had. She'd never thought a goddess of love and beauty would need geography!

"The squiggles and lines at the bottom appear to be a map to Pygmalion's home, as we guessed," said Hathor.

"Ha! We figured that out too!" Artemis told her.

"Why are you so interested in this boy?" Aphrodite demanded. "I'm the one with the Lonely Hearts Club. He was writing to me."

"You don't know that for sure. And you had no right to start such a club without my permission. I'm in charge of all things related to the heart," said Isis. Although she spoke to Aphrodite, once again her eyes darted to Hathor, almost as if she expected her words to be challenged.

"Since the letter doesn't mention either of you by

name, neither of you has the greater claim on it," said Hathor.

"I'm afraid she's right," said Athena.

"Then we'll both go to Cyprus and let Pygmalion say which of us his letter was meant for," said Aphrodite.

"Deal," said Isis. "We can travel on Ra's sunboat."

"Excuse me." Hathor pulled her aside and whispered to her.

Isis blushed. "Oh, I just remembered that it will take all day for the sun to cross the sky."

"We can take my cart," Aphrodite offered. Even though she didn't like Isis for challenging her right to the title of goddessgirl of love, for some reason she felt like she needed to stick up for Isis against Hathor. And that was really dumb. Those two were friends!

"Want us to come with you?" Persephone asked.

Aphrodite thought for a moment. If *her* friends came, Isis's friends would probably insist on coming too. And this conflict was between her and Isis. Besides, her friends deserved to have a vacation. They weren't the ones doing community service! So she shook her head. "No, you all stay here. See the sights. Have some fun. I'll be back as soon as I can."

"What about our bags?" asked Persephone.

"And where will we stay?" asked Athena.

"You'll stay with us," Ma-at told them. "In the dorms at school."

"It's semester break here, so you won't be interfering with classes," added Bastet. Her voice was a soft purr and her eyes were tilted, like her cat's.

"We're on holiday break too," Artemis told her.

As arrangements were made to take her friends' cases to the dorms, Aphrodite said her farewells.

As she hugged Athena, she nodded toward Hathor. "Keep an eye on that one. I don't trust her."

Athena nodded. "I don't think Isis trusts her either."

Within minutes Aphrodite had cast her spell on the swans and stowed her bag in the cart. Then she and Isis were sailing over the Mediterranean Sea toward the island of Cyprus. After a few minutes, Isis pointed to a giant sphere in east Cairo that was as tall as a pyramid. "That's our school."

"Why is it round?"

Isis looked surprised. "It's built in the shape of our illustrious Ra, of course."

Aphrodite stared at her, not understanding.

"Ra—the sun god," said Isis. "He's also our school principal at Ra Academy."

"We go to Mount Olympus Academy. It's on our tallest mountain, high above Greece."

"Is your principal named Olympus?"

Aphrodite shook her head. "No, Zeus. It seems so weird that you don't know anything about us. Where I come from, *everyone* knows us. In fact, they worship us."

"Then we have that in common," said Isis. "Everyone in Egypt worships us, too."

They smiled at each other, and Aphrodite felt a bond forming between them. Then they both seemed to remember they were rivals. At the same time, they turned their heads to look in opposite directions and spent the rest of the journey in silence.

5
Matchmakers

THE TRIP TO CYPRUS DIDN'T TAKE LONG AND
soon they were landing on a bluff overlooking the
Mediterranean Sea. Once Aphrodite and Isis had
hopped out of the cart, it shrank again, and Aphrodite
stowed the figurine in her handbag.

She and Isis unrolled their halves of the letters and

put them together so they could study the whole map again. "Looks like Pygmalion's house is this way," said Isis, pointing toward a stone path.

Aphrodite nodded. "Let's go."

As they walked down the path that ran along the edge of the bluff, a gentle breeze teased at their hair and fluttered the hems of their long gowns. Far below, it rippled the waters of the sea where striped dolphins frolicked with whales. The island of Cyprus was beautiful, with rich green grasses, wild orchids, daisies, and other flowers. The girls passed several red foxes and white hedgehogs with long pink ears. She'd have to bring the others back here sometime so they could enjoy all this natural beauty, thought Aphrodite. Persephone would especially love the flowers, and Artemis, the animals.

"It's so pretty here," breathed Isis. "I wish my friends had come." Aphrodite glanced at her, marveling again at how often they seemed to think alike.

The path took them to a mailbox that had Pygmalion's name painted on it. Beyond it they saw a house. Two curly-horned sheep were grazing on its grass roof. Marble and granite statues of mythical monsters were scattered around the front yard, some with arms or heads that spun around in the wind and others with moving eyeballs or heads that bobbled. Although they were weird, they were beautifully crafted. Yet most were half-buried in weeds and vines that had grown up around them and had birds nesting in them. Beyond the house was a rock quarry.

"He lives by a rock quarry and makes weird yard art?" said Isis, eyeing a bizarre statue that appeared to be half spinning eagle and half bouncing boar. "What kind of boy does that?"

"He's a sculptor," said Aphrodite. "I guess they need a lot of rock. As for the weird art, I guess we'll find out." When they reached the front door, she pulled the cord to ring the little bell attached to it. *Ding-a-ling!*

Isis grinned at her. "Wait till he sees two goddessgirls on his porch!"

"Yeah, that doesn't happen to a mortal every day," said Aphrodite. Quickly, she refreshed her lip gloss and fluffed her long golden hair. Isis brushed her silky hair back over one shoulder and put a hand on her hip. Both posed dramatically, waiting for the door to open so they could be appropriately worshipped.

When the door finally swung open, an annoyed-looking mortal boy with brown hair and eyes stuck his head out. In one hand, he held a chisel.

Aphrodite and Isis waited for him to be suitably impressed by their immortal fabulousness.

But the boy only blinked, then frowned and shook his head. "No, sorry. Go away." *Wham*! He slammed the door in their faces.

Aphrodite and Isis looked at each other in surprise. "How dare he!" they said at the same time.

This time Isis rang the bell. When the boy opened the door, Aphrodite said, "Are you Pyg—I mean, Pygmalion?"

"Look, I told you," he said, sounding even more irritated than before. "You can't model for one of my sculptures. Please stop bothering me!" He slammed the door again.

After they got over the shock of a mortal boy shutting a door in their faces *twice*, they burst into laughter. "He thinks we want to model for him?" Isis gasped when she finally managed to get control of herself.

"Ha ha. Imagine—him, a mere mortal—rejecting goddesses!" said Aphrodite.

"He must be crazy!" said Isis.

For a moment, they were almost like friends, laughing together and rolling their eyes at this silly mortal boy. But before long, Aphrodite again remembered they were competitors. Isis seemed to recall it at the same time and their smiles faded.

Aphrodite pulled the bell again. "Open up, Pyg!"

The door swung open. "Listen, I'm not going to tell you again—" Pyg began.

But this time both goddesses held up their matching halves of his letter. "Did you mail this?" Aphrodite asked.

Tucking his chisel in his belt, he took both halves of

the letter from them, looking surprised. "Yes. Where did you get my letter? And why is it torn?"

"That's how it was delivered to us," said Isis. "We each got half."

"And you think that's *my* fault?" he said, tapping his sandaled foot impatiently. "Why don't you complain to the magic winds? I certainly didn't send it this way." Balling up the entire letter in one hand, he made a show of aiming and shooting it beyond them. It arced high across the front yard and landed right in the open mouth of a stone dragon. "Score!" he said triumphantly.

"We didn't care that it was torn," Aphrodite told him. "We just want to know which one of us you meant to send it to."

"I sent it to the goddess of love," he said. He lowered his voice confidingly, "Because—you'll probably find this hard to believe—but I'm having a little trouble in the crush department."

Both girls spoke at once, saying, "Well, I'm the goddess of love—" They stopped, glaring at each other. They tried again. "And I can help you with that." More glaring.

"Really?" Hope lit Pyg's face as he looked from one to the other. "Both of you are going to help me?"

Isis shook her head, her silky hair swaying. "No."

"But you said—"

"You have to choose one of us," said Aphrodite.

"How am I supposed to do that? I don't even know you. For all I know you're not even goddesses." His eyes widened nervously. "You could be robbers or beasts in disguise!" With that, he started to shut the door on them again.

The nerve of the boy! Aphrodite felt like turning *him*

into a piece of yard art for his impertinence. But then she wouldn't be able to earn the extra credit she needed to improve her Hero-ology grade. "Wait!" she said, slapping her palm on the door to keep it open. Drawing an imaginary circle with her other hand, she quickly showed off her magic, lifting one of his yard sculptures and making it do a fancy series of twirls in the air. Not to be outdone, Isis made it do a final triple-somersault before it settled back down to earth.

Then both girls looked back at him. "Convinced?" Aphrodite asked.

"Okay, so you're goddesses," he relented.

Isis nodded. "And we've come a long way in answer to your letter."

"You *are* still looking for love, aren't you?" Aphrodite asked anxiously.

He blushed. "Well, yeah, sort of."

Isis frowned. "What does that mean?"

Pyg's eyes shifted evasively. But all he said was, "It means I've got work to do. I don't have time to stand around yammering. I need to get hammering!" He pointed to his chisel meaningfully. "Ha ha ha! Get it? That's a sculptor's joke."

Good thing he was a sculptor, thought Aphrodite. He'd never make it as a comedian.

"Come on in if you want," he told them carelessly. Turning around, he headed back inside the house, leaving them to go or stay as they pleased.

Isis's eyes flashed with irritation. Aphrodite knew how she felt. This boy had invited them here, and now he acted like he was doing them a *favor* to let them help him, instead of the other way around. Of course, there was a little bit of truth to that, Aphrodite had to admit. After all, if she succeeded in helping Pyg, it would help her earn a better grade in Hero-ology. Still, it felt as though Pyg was treating her and Isis like servants instead of goddesses. For that, he deserved to be turned into a toad, or worse. But she didn't dare. Isis would win the title of goddess of love for sure then. So she just mumbled sarcastically, "Gosh, thanks so much for your hospitality."

"You're welcome," he said, oblivious to her sarcasm. They trailed him down a dim hall with walls that were carved with fantastic serpents, dragons, fairies, nymphs, and Centaurs. Leftover rock chips crunched under their delicate sandals as they walked. Aphrodite sneezed at the rock dust in the air.

"Is this your work?" asked Isis, gazing around the hallway.

"Uh-huh," he said.

"It's wonderful," said Aphrodite, impressed.

He shrugged. "Yeah, I know," he said matter-of-factly. "I'm famous in the art world."

No false modesty there, thought Aphrodite. She should have guessed that from his letter—since he'd said he was amazing. What kind of girl was going to want an unfunny, clueless, arrogant boy like him? Quickly, she reminded herself that there was someone for everyone.

Finally they reached a large room that was obviously his art studio. Sculpting tools were everywhere and sculptures of all sizes and shapes and subjects stood around the room. Drawn by their beauty, she and Isis walked among them. A tall one near the back was draped with a linen sheet. Aphrodite started to lift the drape for a peek, but jumped away when Pyg ran over and hugged it protectively. "No! It's not finished!" he shrieked.

And they called *her* a diva! "Godness, get over

yourself," Aphrodite murmured under her breath. From the corner of her eye, Isis, who'd overheard her, grinned.

Pyg straightened, looking a little embarrassed at his dramatics. "Sorry. It's just that I don't like anyone to see my work until it's complete."

As if to draw their attention away from the mysterious statue, he grabbed two hunks of balsa wood. "Hey! Watch this!" Whittling quickly, he shaped them with lightning-fast cuts and turns of his tools. Within minutes he was finished and handed them each a figurine.

"Ye gods!" said Aphrodite. He'd made little sculptures of her and Isis exactly as they'd posed to impress him on his porch earlier. Just when she'd decided he was totally hopeless, he'd gone and done something nice. "They're so lifelike," she said, smoothing a finger over the image he'd made of her.

"So real I almost expect them to speak," Isis added.

Was she trying to outdo her with compliments? wondered Aphrodite. Just in case, she declared, "I've never seen anything more beautiful in all of Mount Olympus!"

Isis frowned at her. "Well, *I've* never seen anything more exquisite in all of Egypt!"

Pyg waved a hand, brushing their words away. Taking up his chisel again, he began hacking away at a block of peach-colored stone that was sitting on a worktable. "I know my work is perfection, so no need to flatter me. Just tell me—do you think you can help me?"

"Of course," Aphrodite told him eagerly. "In fact, I've created a quiz for lonely hearts that will help me find you the girl of your dreams."

Pyg flicked a hand in the air. "Quiz schmiz. I hate tests. And I don't have time for that anyway."

111

"But—" Aphrodite protested.

"I won't make you take a quiz," Isis interrupted.

"I didn't say you *had* to take it," said Aphrodite, not wanting him to choose Isis. After all, she'd only created the quiz because she figured it would speed things up in finding love for her club members. "I can find you the girl of your dreams without it. A Greek girl!" Then she added, "The Greeks are the smartest, most talented, beautiful mortals in the world!"

"Egyptians are even smarter, more talented, and more beautiful," Isis insisted. "And we know something about great sculpture, too. Just look at the Sphinx!"

"That was built out of limestone blocks," Aphrodite scoffed. "The Greeks created true sculpture, carved from stone. Our Colossus of Rhodes and the new statue of Zeus at Olympia are among the seven ancient wonders of the world!"

"Oh, yeah? Well, so is the Great Pyramid," Isis was quick to say.

"Whoa!" Pyg held up a hand. "Why are you both trying so hard to impress me?"

"Because half of your letter was delivered to each of us—" Isis began.

"But only one of us can be the true goddess of love," Aphrodite added quickly. "And that's me." Her eyes challenged Isis.

"I don't think so," Isis countered ferociously.

They both swung back to look at him. "So which of us do you choose?" Aphrodite demanded.

Pyg's brown eyes sparkled with mischief. "You mean *I* get to decide which of you is the true goddessgirl of love? Woo-hoo! This is going to be fun!"

Aphrodite and Isis glanced at each other, worried by the gleam in his eye.

"Hmm. Let me see. Who should I choose?" Waving the tip of his chisel back and forth between the two of them he chanted, "Genie, meeny, goddess, goo. I think that I'll choose . . . *both* of you!"

"Huh?" Aphrodite and Isis exclaimed at the same time.

Pyg grinned at them in excitement. "We'll make it a contest to see who gets to be the one and only true goddess of love. Won't that be a hoot? Whoever brings me the girl of my dreams wins. Agreed?"

Aphrodite scowled at him, but what could she do? Win the contest, that's what! "Agreed," she said after a moment's hesitation.

"I'm in," said Isis.

"Okey dokey, then," said Pyg. "I've got work to do. And so do you! So let's all get cracking." With that, he ushered them back through his house toward his front door. "How long do you think it'll take you to find my new crush?" he asked on the way.

"Maybe two m—" Isis began.

"Two minutes would be fantastic," he said, pleased.

Isis raised her brows. "I was going to say two *months*!"

Pyg shook his head. "Nuh-uh. Way too long. How about two hours? Deal?"

"You're joking, right?" said Aphrodite. She really was itching to turn him into a toad. Or maybe smite him. Or both.

"Two weeks?" Isis countered.

"Okay, two days it is," said Pyg, opening the front door for them.

Aphrodite and Isis looked at each other in consternation. Two days wasn't enough time to find true love for anyone!

"You can each bring me three crush candidates,"

Pygmalion said as the girls stepped out onto the porch. "And if one of them turns out to be perfect for me, I'll declare whoever brought her to be the true goddess of love." He gave them a cocky farewell salute. "Later!" Then he shut the door in their faces. Again.

"Two days? This is hopeless," said Aphrodite, shaking her head.

"Does that mean you give up?" asked Isis.

Aphrodite straightened, remembering what was at stake. "No way. You?"

"No," said Isis. "So I guess we'll meet back here in two days?"

"Right," said Aphrodite. "Want a ride back to Cairo before I fly home?"

Isis shook her head, the beads in her shiny, smooth

hair clicking gently. "Ra's sunboat is just over there," she said, pointing toward the setting sun. "I can get a ride from him."

"Then I guess I'll head back to Greece," said Aphrodite. "Would you mind taking a message to my goddessgirl friends in Cairo?"

"Not at all," Isis replied graciously. Aphrodite pulled a blank piece of papyrus from her handbag and scribbled out a note explaining what was going on. Isis took it, then they each went their separate ways.

Moments later, as Aphrodite's swans lifted her golden cart into the air and started toward MOA, she watched Isis step into a long boat that also held the setting sun. A muscled god was at the helm, slowly steering it to where the sea and sky met. All around it, the sky turned scarlet, pink, and gold. Just before the boat disappeared on the horizon, Isis turned her head and glanced toward Aphrodite, a determined look in her eye.

Aphrodite met her gaze with a determined look of her own. If Isis thought she could beat her at the game of love, she had another think coming!

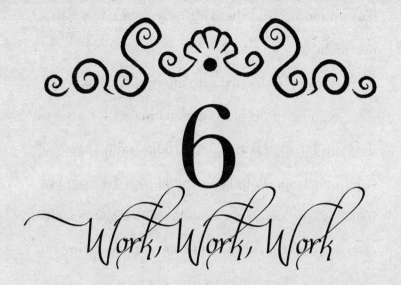

6
Work, Work, Work

THE MINUTE SHE LANDED IN THE MOA COURT-
yard, Aphrodite spotted Pheme coming down the
granite stairs toward her. Quickly, she shrank her
swan cart and waved the girl over.

"I'm so glad to see you. I have new news!" Aphrodite
told her, dragging her travel case behind her. She
sure wished she'd packed lighter, especially since it

had wound up that she hadn't even stayed in Cairo overnight!

Pheme's eyes widened with interest. "Do tell."

"I'm going to be playing matchmaker for a very, um, special mortal boy," Aphrodite said. "And I'll need your help." Pulling a sheet of papyrus from her handbag, she sat on the bottom step of MOA's staircase and began writing. This time she was taking no chances that Pheme might garble her message.

"What's this boy's name?" Pheme asked eagerly as she sat down beside her. "Is he rich? Handsome? Smart? Funny? Where does he live?"

"Sorry, I can't reveal the details," said Aphrodite as she wrote. If she did, girls might go straight to Pyg's house to meet him on their own. No, she must be the one to present them to him. Then, when he fell in love with one of them, he would proclaim her the one and *only* goddessgirl of love! She paused in her writing to imagine the scene of her triumph, with trumpets blaring and cheering crowds waving colorful flags. Would she wear her ruby-red chiton or her new aquamarine one? Red, she decided. "But I will say this," she went on, pushing her daydream aside for now. "This boy is a real Lonely Heart looking for love."

"Oh, he sounds adorable! And fascinating," said Pheme, obviously intrigued.

"And I plan to help him find a new crush by holding a competition," Aphrodite continued. "That's where you come in. I want you to spread the word about it. Tell the mortal maidens in Greece to come to the agora in Athens tomorrow morning if they'd like to compete for this special boy's favor. I'll interview them and then choose three girls for my client's consideration."

"The three prettiest?" asked Pheme.

"Not necessarily." Having finished writing, Aphrodite used the end of her quill pen to poke a hole in the top two corners of the papyrus square. Pulling a gold chain from her case, she strung it through the holes. "I will choose the three I judge to be the most suitable for the particular boy I have in mind." Which meant finding a girl who was extremely tolerant of boys who were clueless, annoying, and boastful. A tall order. At least he was talented. She'd just have to find girls who appreciated that and could overlook the rest. There was someone for everyone, she kept reminding herself.

Just then, they spotted Hermes walking across the courtyard toward his delivery chariot with an armload of packages. Pheme jumped up and waved wildly at him. "Wait up!" Before she could dash off, Aphrodite grabbed the back of her chiton to stop her. Pheme tugged at her dress, trying to escape. "Let go! Don't you want me to start spreading your news? I have to hurry if I'm going to catch a ride to Greece with Hermes."

"First, I want you to promise me you'll wear this the whole time you're in Greece, okay?" said Aphrodite. Standing, she looped the gold chain around Pheme's neck and clasped it, so that the papyrus sign she'd made hung in front of the girl's chest.

Without even reading what Aphrodite had written, Pheme nodded. "I promise." The sign was only an announcement of the details of the competition, but it could have been a KICK ME sign for all Pheme knew. She was in such a panic to spread her gossip that she rushed off as soon as Aphrodite let her go, dashing toward Hermes' chariot as if her sandals were on fire. Still, Aphrodite was comforted by the fact that no matter how Pheme messed up the spoken news this time, everyone would know the true details of the contest by reading her sign.

Picking up her travel case, Aphrodite dragged it up the steps toward the school building, huffing and puffing. Normally several godboys would have dropped everything in their eagerness to help her, but as luck would have it there wasn't a single godboy in sight. Many were gone for the holiday, and since she could hear Apollo's band practicing upstairs in the fifth floor boys' dorm, those who were still here were probably upstairs listening, completely unaware that she needed help!

"I give you an *E* for *e*ffort," Medusa joked. Aphrodite glanced up to see the green girl standing a few steps above her clutching a scroll and blocking her path.

"I'll give you one back for excuse me," said Aphrodite.

Medusa moved, then fell into step beside Aphrodite as she continued climbing the stairs. Medusa lightly tapped the end of her scroll against the side of her leg as she walked. "And speaking of grades, you never did say what you made in Hero-ology."

Aphrodite dropped her bag on the top step and glared at her, feeling tired and frustrated. "Ye gods! I got a B," she fibbed, spreading her arms wide. "Satisfied?"

Medusa's snakes hissed, as if they were *sssuspiciousss* that Aphrodite wasn't telling the truth. Medusa arched an eyebrow, as if she didn't quite believe her either. "If you say so, drama queen."

She didn't know why, but for some reason Medusa

had had it in for her almost since first grade. Suddenly fed up with her name-calling, Aphrodite asked bluntly, "Why don't you like me?"

Startled by her directness, Medusa's eyes went wide. For once she didn't have a snarky—or snaky—comeback.

"Is it because I'm immortal and you're not? Or because I'm popular?" asked Aphrodite.

"No!" Medusa shot her an angry stare, then blurted. "It's because you're so happy."

"Happy?" Of all the things she'd expected Medusa to say, this was not on the list.

Medusa nodded. "It's annoying. You're always looking on the bright side and seeing possibilities for love everywhere. *Bleah!*" She opened her mouth and pointed inside it, pretending to gag, then ranted on. "Everything's so easy for you just because you're pretty. You don't even have to try and boys adore you. You're not even smart and teachers give you good grades. It's not fair."

Not smart? There it was again, the implication that she was dumb! Aphrodite stepped back as if she'd been struck by a blow. Then she just lost it. "Do I look happy to you?" she yelled, not even caring that her scowl might be giving her wrinkles at the moment

If only Medusa knew the truth—that Zeus and Mr. Cyclops were upset with her. That her claim to the title of goddess of love was in danger, and that she'd made a D in Hero-ology. She wasn't about to confess all that, though, so instead she said, "I assure you things are *not* as easy for me as you imagine!"

"Oh, go tell your sob story to someone who's interested," scoffed Medusa. It was obvious she didn't believe Aphrodite, or at least thought she was exaggerating—

playing the diva role again. "Here." Slapping the scroll she held into Aphrodite's palm, she stalked off.

Realizing it was the Lonely Hearts Club quiz she'd dropped by Medusa's room that morning, Aphrodite tucked it under one arm and continued dragging her bag. Had she really expected any sympathy from Medusa?

When she got to her room, she found Pandora's quiz half-shoved under her door. However, there were no more letters in her Lonely Hearts mailbox. That made her success in helping Pyg more important than ever. Everything hinged on it. It was her only chance to regain her title and the favor of mortals, to calm Zeus, and to make Mr. Cyclops view her community service as a success and agree to improve her grade. She had to win, or forever be a loser!

She tossed her bag on her spare bed and set the swan

cart figurine back on its shelf. She was exhausted! And hungry. Taking the two quizzes with her, she headed to the cafeteria. She had no intention of helping Medusa after what she'd just said, but she was still curious to see how the two mortal girls had responded. Sitting down with a carton of nectar and a heaping plate of ambrosia salad and cloud nine soup, she began reviewing their quizzes.

Several of the questions had been written with her best friends in mind. For example, when she'd asked what kind of animal they liked, she was thinking of Artemis.

Pandora had answered: *?* to that one. In fact, she'd written question marks as answers to several questions. Aphrodite supposed that shouldn't have come as a surprise, considering.

Medusa had answered: *reptile* to the animal

question. Also unsurprising. Considering.

She glanced at some of the girls' other answers to the mostly multiple choice questions:

What do you love most about yourself? (Please check one.)

☐ *I have a good personality.*

☐ *I'm smart.*

☐ *I'm a good friend.*

☐ *I'm pretty (or handsome).*

☐ *My creativity.*

☐ *I can keep a secret.*

☐ *Other* _____

Pandora had checked "other" and in the blank beside it, she'd written: *That I'm curious?*

Medusa had checked all six responses, and beside "Other" she'd written: *I'm green.*

Aphrodite bit back a giggle at Medusa's answer. She

may have checked all the responses, but after what she'd just said to Aphrodite, it was easy to guess that she wasn't nearly as self-confident as she pretended to be. Feeling eyes on her, she glanced around. The cafeteria seemed practically empty now that so many students had gone on holiday. She tried not to feel too sorry for herself that they were off having fun, while she was here working.

Three tables away, she saw Pandora sitting beside Hephaestus's crush, Aglaia. Pandora waved when she caught her eye. Aphrodite smiled, but didn't invite the two girls over. Pandora's constant questions would keep her from being able to read over the quizzes! At another table, Medusa sat with her two sisters. When she caught her eye, Medusa glanced away, looking suddenly shy. Shy? Medusa?

Her club was important to these two mortals,

Aphrodite realized with surprise. Both girls were honest-to-goodness Lonely Hearts and were hoping she could help them connect with someone who would like them. Feeling touched, she studied the quizzes more closely. Mr. Cyclops might not think Medusa and Pandora counted as far as her grade went, but they still needed her help! Quickly, she read the girls' answers to the rest of the quiz, which included questions like:

How would your friends describe you?

What makes you a good catch?

How would you describe your ideal boyfriend?

Pandora's answer to the last question was: *Maybe a godboy who likes water and has turquoise skin?*

Medusa's answer was: *A godboy with turquoise skin who likes fountains, oceans, and tridents.*

Uh-oh! There was only one boy in all of MOA with turquoise skin, and that was *Poseidon.*

Actually, Aphrodite wasn't *that* surprised. She'd guessed that Medusa and Pandora were both crushing on Poseidon a long time ago and this just proved she'd been right. Pandora asked Poseidon more questions than she asked anyone else, and Medusa often stuck up for him. Those were the kinds of little details a goddess-girl of love noted and remembered.

Aphrodite looked around for Poseidon. He was sitting at another table, laughing and joking with his buddies, Apollo, Ares, and Dionysus. They'd finished their lunches and were building some kind of tower out of textscrolls, plates, nectar cartons, and various other random items on their trays. She noticed Pandora and Medusa both looking at him with identical looks of adoration.

Yet Poseidon, she was sure, was totally unaware that two girls were in like with him. Godboys were so dense sometimes. Or maybe Poseidon just didn't like them the way they liked him, and so was trying not to encourage them. Aphrodite rubbed her forehead. She was too tired to figure this out tonight.

As she took her tray to the counter, she noticed a poster on the bulletin board nearby. Something about Apollo's band, Heavens Above, playing at a dance. Oh, yeah, she'd forgotten about that. It was an MOA tradition to mark the end of Hero Week with a dance in which everyone dressed in hero costumes.

"Are you going?" It was Artemis's twin brother, Apollo. He, Dionysus, and Ares had come up behind her to toss their trash.

Dionysus gestured toward the sign on the board. "To the Hero Dance at the end of the week," he said. "Our band's playing."

"Well, I love dances," she began.

Apollo laughed. "We know."

"And I love your band." She smiled at the godboys, trying to smother a yawn. "I'm kind of busy, but I'll come by for a while at least." A dance was the last thing she should be thinking about right now, but she wanted to be supportive and she did like their music.

"Promise?" asked Ares. "We stayed at MOA during the holiday just so we could polish our new songs in time." Aphrodite looked up at him. Had he grown another inch or two in the last week or so? And gotten even cuter? Even though they'd broken up for good, her heart did its familiar pitter-patter. Was he having second thoughts about the breakup? "And it'd be great if you could bring your friends, too," he added, bursting her bubble.

"Ares just joined the band and he wants lots of girls around to admire him," Dionysus teased.

So that was it, Aphrodite thought as Ares gave his arm a mock punch. "Sure, okay, I'll spread the word," she said. "See you guys later."

Once in her room, she fell asleep the minute her head hit her heart-shaped pillow.

The next morning, after unpacking her case, showering, dressing, and having a quick breakfast, she enchanted her cart once again and flew down to Greece. She landed in Athens, the city named after Athena of course, and immediately noticed that there was a long queue at the Agora Marketplace. Girls were lined up from one end of the colonnaded building to the other, their line even snaking around the back. *There must be a big sale*, she thought, wishing she had time to join them in their shopping.

"You're here!" As Aphrodite tucked her figurine

into her handbag, Pheme hurried toward her. "Great turnout, huh?" She gestured toward the agora.

Aphrodite's jaw dropped. "You mean all those girls are here for my competition?"

Pheme nodded, looking proud. "Once everyone heard that you were competing with some hoity-toity Egyptian goddess to determine who'd be crowned the goddessgirl of love, they—"

Aphrodite's breath caught and she grabbed Pheme's arm. "I never told you that! How did you find out about Isis?"

"You didn't tell me?" Pheme looked confused.

"No, I didn't."

"Well, then, I must have picked up the information somewhere else," said Pheme, shrugging. "Oh! Now I remember. I heard it from the friend of a friend who knows that friend's brother's girlfriend who lives in Egypt, who heard it from—"

"Never mind," said Aphrodite. She couldn't help feeling embarrassed that the whole world knew about the challenge to her status as the one and only goddess of love! Why did Pheme have to have such a big mouth?

Still, she held her head high as she and Pheme walked toward the agora. She couldn't worry about what people thought of her now. She had to concentrate on interviewing candidates to find a crush for Pyg. A delicate golden chair with a pink velvet seat cushion had been placed on a granite pedestal, waiting for her. Next to it stood a tall crystal vase of long-stemmed red roses. And next to that, someone had set an easel with a fancy sign upon it that read:

Today only!
Meet: Aphrodite,
the one and only true goddess of love.
Compete in her
Mortal Matchmaker contest!

"How nice!" she said, admiring the preparations. The minute she sat down, a mortal girl brought her a jeweled goblet of iced nectar. A minute later, two more girls came to stand on either side of her chair, and began to gently fan her with enormous palm leaves. Wow! This was certainly the royal treatment. What was going on? She'd thought mortals were mad at her!

The queue was long and she wanted to get to everyone today, so Aphrodite waved the first two girls in line forward. She'd brought a notescroll with a copy of her quiz questions and blank pages for taking notes, which she set on her lap.

At her summons, the girls curtsied and then approached her. "Your hair is so beautiful," said one of them, sounding surprised.

"Yes, it grew back amazingly fast!" said her friend.

"What?" Aphrodite asked, automatically smoothing a hand over her lustrous hair.

"Well, I heard you had a fight with Isis and she pulled out half of your hair," said the first girl.

"I heard the same thing," said the second girl, "only I heard you were bald now. Is that a wig?"

"No! It is not a wig," Aphrodite huffed. What a way to start things! "Thank you for your time, ladies." She looked down the line. "Next!"

Two more girls stepped forward.

"Where are the scratches?" asked one before

Aphrodite could speak. "I heard that Isis has finger-nails three inches long and she scratched your arms to ribbons."

"No, I heard she scratched your face," said the other.

"Neither is true, as you can see," said Aphrodite.

"But she did call you a twit, right?"

"I heard it was a two-faced twit," said the other girl.

"Once and for all—Isis and I did not have a fight!" she said a bit more loudly than she'd intended. For a moment the two mortals looked startled, but then they nodded. Even so, Aphrodite wasn't sure they believed her. Recalling that she was here to appease mortals, not argue with them, she managed to smile. "Thank you for coming, girls. Next!"

As they turned to go, one of them glanced back at Aphrodite. "Good luck," she said. "Maybe you don't know it, but everyone came today because we all want you to win. After all, you are one of us—a *Greek*! And we believe that you and only you are the true goddess of love."

Aphrodite stared after her, and a warm, happy feeling filled her chest. She hadn't wanted it to get out that Isis had challenged her right to the title of goddess of love. But now that it had, she could see it was actually a *good* thing. Hearing the news, these mortals had had an instant change of heart about her. Amazing! They'd been won over to her side in less than a day!

7

Godboys and Pyramids

As the line moved along, Aphrodite met hundreds of girls. Many of them had everything going for them—brains, good personalities, talent, and beauty. But she didn't choose these girls for Pyg. Instead, she directed them to a message board where she'd had Pheme post a copy of her quiz. She told them to send their answers to her at MOA, promising that she would work on finding them true love and get back to them.

Toward afternoon, some of the godboys from MOA showed up. Apparently, Apollo, Dionysus, Ares, Eros, and Poseidon had heard about the competition and had come by to get in on the fun. She wished they hadn't, because they were distracting the mortal girls. The five of them hung around in the nearby field roughhousing and showing off their godboy skills. It was their way of flirting.

Apollo and Eros were practicing their archery, trying to impress the girls with their perfect bull's-eyes. Ares and Poseidon were arm wrestling to show off their bulging muscles. And Dionysus, wearing a blindfold, was wandering around trying to "accidentally" bump into girls. On the blindfold, he'd written: LOVE IS

BLIND. *Sometimes it is, and sometimes it isn't,* thought Aphrodite.

Still, the boys were all so handsome and intriguing that the mortal girls were watching them instead of listening to her. When she'd had enough, she told the girls in line to take a break. Then she stomped over to confront the godboys. "I'm trying to work here," she told them.

"We're not stopping you!" said Ares, grinning at her. The sun gleamed on his wavy blond hair as he picked up a shimmery godball they'd brought from MOA and prepared to throw it. His four friends ran into the field, ready to intercept. "We heard you were planning to start another war, so we wanted to come watch," he added, his eyes twinkling with laughter.

"What is that supposed to mean?" she demanded as

he let the ball fly. As it zigzagged, did a figure eight, and then flew sideways, the other godboys chased it.

Ares gazed at her speculatively. "You and your friend Isis have started something with this competition. Mortals all over earth are rooting for their favorite goddess. Some favor you. Some favor her."

"So everyone's enthusiastic. What's wrong with that?"

"There are bound to be arguments." He pointed toward a scuffle going on a distance away. He was right! Even now, several mortals were fighting over who should win—her or Isis! "If you're chosen, the Egyptians will be mad. If Isis is, the Greeks will be," he added.

Aphrodite recalled one of Ms. Nemesis's lessons in Revenge-ology class: *Insult a goddess and you insult those who worship her.* Greeks were certainly taking that to heart. It appeared she was in a no-win situation.

"So I'm right back to where I started," she murmured, forgetting Ares was standing there.

"What?" he asked. Having caught the ball, Apollo and the other godboys drew near, ready to start another game, but Ares waved them off. He put a hand on her arm. "What's wrong? Did one of these mortals say something to offend you?" His eyes narrowed and his hands balled into fists. He glanced around, looking ready to punish whomever she named.

"No, nothing like that," she said with a quick shake of her head.

"Then what?" She looked up into his concerned blue eyes. She and Ares had had their ups and downs and he had said things that had hurt her in the past. But right now he seemed so kind and strong, and . . . and *trustworthy*. Like she could tell him anything. Before she knew it, she was admitting the truth about her grade, Pyg, and everything. "I know you enjoy battle, but I feel bad about starting the Trojan incident. My actions caused a lot of trouble for mortals."

He grinned. "Trojan *incident?*"

Smiling, she elbowed him gently. He made an *oof* sound and pretended to be hurt, then smiled back at her and took her hand in his. "Thanks for telling me. I care about you, you know?"

"Woo woo!" called Eros, zeroing in on the hand-holding from downfield where the boys were still tossing around the ball. Dionysus put his little fingers between his lips and whistled. Apollo and Poseidon started making kissing noises.

Aphrodite glared at them and stepped back from Ares so he dropped her hand. "Ye gods—are they in first grade? Can you get them out of here? They're distracting the girls from my matchmaking competition."

"Sure," said Ares. "Anything for you." Blue eyes sparkling with humor, he trotted off to join his friends.

As she headed back to the agora, Aphrodite peeked toward the field just in time to see Ares glance her way, then say something to the other godboys that made them laugh. She turned away, suddenly embarrassed and a little angry. Had he made a joke about her requesting the boys to leave? What if she'd been wrong to trust him? Maybe he was even telling them what she'd confessed! She hadn't told him not to, but he should know better!

Minutes later the godboys began loosening the wings on their sandals and were soon moving off in the direction of MOA. So Ares had succeeded in convincing them to leave at least. She sighed. Just when you thought you had godboys figured out, you didn't.

She had only been apart from her goddessgirl friends for one day, but she already missed them. Although she hoped they were having fun, she also wished they were here. Talking things over with them would be so helpful.

Still, they were probably having fun and she was not going to interrupt their vacation. She'd tell them everything later, once she'd succeeded in changing her grade. She imagined how they'd all laugh about it then. For now, though, it wasn't so funny because her success wasn't assured. Yet. This competition was hers to win or lose. Taking her seat on the golden chair again, she smiled at the girl at the front of the line. "Next."

Meanwhile, back in Egypt, the other goddessgirls were heading from Cairo toward the pyramids of Giza. Athena took the lead of their small caravan riding on a butter-colored camel with Hathor. Behind them, Persephone rode on a dark brown one with Ma'at; while Artemis shared a white one with Bastet. Each pair of goddesses sat atop a colorful saddle that was designed to protect the tall hump on their camel's back.

As they passed through the bazaar on their way, Athena noticed a long line of girls streaming from a large tent. "What's going on over there?" she asked.

"Oh, nothing," Hathor replied evasively. "Did you bring the map?"

"Yes," said Athena. She forgot all about the line of girls as she tried to plan the best route. Reading the map wasn't easy—camel rides were bumpy! "Giza is west of Cairo through the Sahara desert," she said at last. "It looks like we're going the right way."

"Don't worry," Hathor replied, her body rolling easily with each step and sway of the camel. "I've been to the pyramids a mummillion times. We won't get lost."

Athena thought about asking exactly how much a mummillion amounted to, and if it was even a real number. And why had Hathor asked her to check the map if she already knew the way? But just then, Persephone interrupted. "Are we there yet?" she asked, half-jokingly, fanning herself with her hands. "I already feel like a wilted pansy."

"You'll get used to the heat after a while," said Ma'at. "Egypt and most of northern Africa is desert. That's why we rode out so early this morning. But don't worry—we'll stay inside as much as we can when we reach the pyramids."

"You mean we can go inside them?" Athena asked, overhearing.

"Of course. We're goddesses," Hathor said in a snooty tone. "And in your honor, the pyramids are closed to mortals today. We'll have them all to ourselves."

At the rear of their caravan, Artemis and Bastet were busy talking about one of their favorite subjects—animals. "Is it true that camels store water in their humps?" asked Artemis.

Bastet burst out laughing. "No!"

"Then how do they go so long without drinking?"

"They have adapted to survive in the desert. They don't sweat as much as horses, and their coats help reflect sunlight." Her cat wasn't perched on her shoulder today. She'd left it in the dorm, explaining to Artemis that her cat hated camel rides.

An hour later, they came up over a sand dune, and suddenly the three pyramids of Giza stood majestically before them. Athena's camel made a loud and long sound that was somewhere between a snore and a honk, as if to announce their arrival.

"That one's the Great Pyramid of Pharaoh Khufu!" said Athena. "I recognize it from one of the travel brochures."

"Correct," said Hathor. "It's the oldest and largest of the three pyramids."

Bastet gave her camel a command so she and Artemis could dismount. The camel bent its front legs, going to its knees. Its entire body tilted forward.

"Whoa!" said Artemis, as she fell forward with the motion. "This feels weird."

"Don't worry, you won't fall off," said Bastet. The camel rocked backward then, bending its back legs under it. Then it rocked forward again and settled down until it was lying on its belly with all four legs folded underneath.

Bastet swung from the saddle and stepped down, and Artemis did as well. Copying them, the others dismounted too. Then they all headed for the pyramids. By the time they reached the entrance, the wax cone on Ma'at's head had begun to melt, releasing a pleasing spicy fragrance. Seeing Persephone's curiosity, she explained that this was the way Egyptians perfumed themselves.

"You see before you the Grand Gallery," Hathor announced grandly, as they stepped inside the Great Pyramid. "We're using it for an exhibit of hieroglyphs this month," she added, leading them up an incline.

Once their eyes got used to the darkness, Persephone peered closely at some of the hieroglyphs hanging on the gallery walls. Spying a blue flower with pointed leaves on one panel, she smiled. "A blue lotus!"

Ma'at nodded, coming to stand by her. "It's a symbol of rebirth. Because at night the lotus closes and sinks underwater. Then at dawn it rises and opens again."

"I wonder if a lotus could grow in the River Styx in the Underworld. The flower is so beautiful and the Underworld can be so dreary," mused Persephone.

Ma'at looked as if she had a question, but before she could ask it, Hathor waved them on. "This way to the Queen's Chamber," she told them.

"Will the queen mind us barging in?" asked Artemis.

Bastet giggled. "I doubt it. She's long dead—a mummy now. Robbers looted these pyramids long ago. The gold treasures and artifacts are gone, but the pyramids still remain as great monuments."

After they stepped inside the Queen's Chamber, Ma'at pointed to a feather symbol among the hieroglyphs on the walls. "That is my symbol," she said.

"There's a hieroglyph just for you?" Athena asked, impressed.

"There's one for each of us," said Hathor. She pointed to a symbol of a bird in a square. "This one's mine."

"I'm even in the Book of the Dead," Ma'at added proudly. She took them to a book set upon a pedestal. "The book doesn't mention the Underworld you describe, Persephone. Therefore, it must not exist."

"It does too. I've been there!" Persephone insisted. "It's where my crush lives and where the dead hang out."

All three Egyptian goddesses gasped. "You're wrong," said Hathor, folding her arms.

"Death is the beginning of a journey to the Afterlife," said Bastet. "Everyone knows that."

Ma'at nodded. "At the beginning of such a journey,

my feather helps weigh whether someone was good or bad in life. See?" She pointed to a scene on the wall in which a feather was being used as a weight on one side of a hanging scale. "And if you are good, the Book of the Dead will offer you the magic spells needed to pass into the Afterlife."

"But—" Persephone began, ready to argue.

"Perhaps we should move on," said Athena, tugging at her arm.

"Uh, right," said Persephone. She forced herself to smile politely at Ma'at. "I guess that, in matters of the Underworld, we'll just have to agree to disagree."

After a minute, Ma'at gave her a small nod. "But I hope we can still be friends in spite of our disagreement, yes?" Persephone sent her a warm smile in return. "Yes." Friends didn't have to agree on everything, after all.

Hathor stepped back into the hall. "Follow me to the King's Chamber."

As they entered the next chamber, Artemis felt something brush her leg. Letting out a squeal, she grabbed at Bastet. "What was that?" She was brave about many things, but this room was just plain spooky! Glancing down, she saw that a white cat had appeared out of nowhere. Then she noticed that several more were slinking around the chamber as well. They acted as if they owned it!

"Don't worry," said Bastet, as if there was nothing unusual about seeing cats in the pyramids. "They won't hurt you."

Hathor smirked, then began showing the others around the chamber.

"What is it with all the cats around here?" Artemis muttered, attempting to cover up her embarrassment.

"That shop I went to in the bazaar had shelves and shelves of cat statues, cat-shaped bowls, cat earrings—"

"Do you have something against cats?" Bastet interrupted. A gray one paused nearby and looked up at Artemis, as if it wanted to hear her reply too.

"Not really." Artemis shrugged. "I've just never been around them much. I have dogs." On the ground nearby, the gray cat stretched its front legs out, showing its claws. Artemis eyed it warily.

"It's okay to pet her. The tour guides feed them and they're all tame," said Bastet. "Don't be scared."

"I'm not!" said Artemis. To prove it, she knelt and commanded, "Here, kitty, kitty." But the cat ignored her and began licking its front paw with a pink tongue. Artemis looked up at Bastet. "Why won't it come? My dogs always come when I call. Well, most of the time."

Bastet shrugged. "I suppose it's because cats are smarter than dogs."

Artemis stood abruptly. "I don't think so."

"It's true!" Bastet insisted. "Cats come only when they wish to. Dogs dumbly obey."

"Dogs are not dumb!" As heat rose in Artemis's cheeks, Athena and Persephone came up behind her and gently hooked their arms through hers.

"I'm sure she didn't mean to imply that dogs are dumb," said Persephone. "Right, Bastet?"

Bastet looked anxious. "Actually, I have never been around dogs very much. I didn't mean to give insult in any case. We can remain friends as Persephone and Ma'at have agreed to, even though we disagree?"

A slow smile spread over Artemis's face. "Deal. Maybe sometime you can visit me at MOA and meet my dogs."

Bastet smiled back. "Maybe so."

"Our tour is complete," Hathor announced after they'd been through every tunnel and examined every display. "Shall we return to Cairo?"

All six goddesses retraced their steps and exited the Great Pyramid, then set off on their return trip by camel. When they reached Cairo, they passed the bazaar again. The line of girls streaming from the large tent they'd seen earlier had shortened. Now they could read a sign that sat on an easel at the tent's entrance:

CALLING ALL EGYPTIAN GIRLS:

HELP ISIS BEAT APHRODITE

IN THE MORTAL MATCHMAKER COMPETITION!

"What's going on over there?" Athena asked.

"Isis is interviewing mortal girls for that contest she and Aphrodite are having," said Hathor. "And now you'll have to excuse us. The three of us promised to help her."

Ma'at and Bastet shared a look. From their expressions, it appeared that they didn't quite trust Hathor and thought she might be up to something.

"But if Isis is here, where's Aphrodite?" asked Persephone.

"She must have gone back to Greece," Athena guessed. "She's probably doing the same thing. Interviewing girls that Pygmalion might like. But why didn't she tell us?"

Hathor grinned. "You are every bit as brainy as they say, Athena. As a matter of fact, I almost forgot." She pulled a note from her pocket. "Isis asked me to give you this. It's from your little friend—Aphroditty."

Taking the note, Athena glared at her. "Her name is Aphro*dite*," she said, as the three goddessgirls quickly scanned the message.

"If they're going to help Isis," said Persephone, glancing at the three Egyptian goddesses, "we should go help Aphrodite."

"Yeah, let's go get our stuff," said Artemis. She, Athena, and Persephone turned to go.

"Sorry, but the only transportation available is Ra's sunboat," said Bastet. "And that left on its trip across the sky this morning. It won't return until tomorrow at dawn."

Athena gasped. "You didn't forget to give us Aphrodite's note, you withheld it on purpose!" she accused. "You *wanted* us to miss the boat!"

Bastet shook her head, looking truly surprised.

But Hathor only shrugged. "All's fair in a contest. Now if you will excuse us, we have to go help Isis win. Come on, girls."

Bastet and Ma'at hesitated as if they felt guilty. "You

must forgive Hathor. Sometimes she doesn't play fair," Ma'at murmured. "Still, she is our friend and wants the best for Isis," said Bastet. Then the two of them nodded in farewell and left for the tent.

"That Hathor makes me so mad," said Athena, when they were gone.

"Me, too," Persephone agreed. "It sounds like the others weren't in on her deception."

"But I hate to think of Aphrodite all alone in Greece, trying to do everything on her own," said Artemis. "I hope she doesn't think we've abandoned her."

"I have a feeling Aphrodite's been holding back on us," said Athena. "There's more to this story than we know."

Persephone nodded. "Let's hope she'll tell us when we finally see her again."

8

Pygmalion's Choice

BACK IN ATHENS, APHRODITE STOOD ON THE steps of the agora, preparing to announce the names of the three Greek girls she'd chosen to visit Pyg. Finding candidates who might please the odd and arrogant boy had been difficult since he hadn't taken her quiz and she knew little about him. Still, she believed that the three she'd picked represented her best chance.

A huge crowd had gathered at the bottom of the marble stairs below her. Some were girls who'd entered the contest, but most were Athenian citizens who'd come to cheer them on. And of course, many were there simply to see Aphrodite herself. After all, it wasn't every day that a goddess visited earth!

"Thank you all for participating in my matchmaker competition," she said in a clear voice that was strong enough to carry. There were few things she enjoyed more than having an audience, and she intended to give these mortals a show today. "This wasn't an easy selection," she went on, "but in the end I could choose only three candidates. If I do not call your name, please don't give up hope of finding your own perfect match. That right person may be just around the corner."

She gestured toward Pheme, who stood next to several baskets full of quizscrolls tied with ribbons.

"And if you'd like my help in finding that right person," Aphrodite continued, "please be sure to fill out one of my quizzes." At that, there were murmurs in the crowd and several people who hadn't entered the competition wandered over to begin filling out quizscrolls.

A male voice called out, "Can a mortal guy fill out a quiz too?"

"Of course," she called back, and the youth and some of his friends headed toward Pheme to grab quizzes. The two goddessgirls had run out of blank ones yesterday, so scribes had worked through the night to have more copies ready for today. Judging by the stack that had already been filled out, mortals seemed more than willing to work with Aphrodite to find love. Obviously, their feelings toward her had softened. Mr. Cyclops was sure to boost her grade when he heard! And if she could win the contest with Pyg, that would be the cherry on top. Maybe this would even get Zeus out of his bad mood, she thought, feeling pleased with herself. Medusa had gotten one thing right about her. She did like looking at the bright side!

Ares' worries about another war seemed distant today as the crowds cheered her on. Surely mortals wouldn't fight over something as silly as a mortal boy's choice between an Egyptian or a Greek crush!

"Now, after I call your names, will the following three maidens please come forward?" Aphrodite said, her voice ringing out again. She knew she looked stunning today, even for a goddess. Her golden hair gleamed, her jewels sparkled, and her brilliant white chiton was the newest style. Posing for effect, she waited a few beats and then called the first name: "Tessa!" There was a squeal of delight from the girl she'd summoned, immediately followed by the cheers of her friends and family. Aphrodite waited until a hush fell over the crowd again before announcing the next name. "Chloe!" Another squeal and more clapping. Finally the crowd quieted again. Aphrodite paused, causing everyone to hold their breath, as they anxiously awaited the last name. "And finally—Zoe!"

Each of the chosen girls hugged her parents, stepped from the audience, and came toward Aphrodite, waving her permission slip for the required travel to Cyprus. The onlookers clapped and cheered as if the girls were heroes.

Once the applause died down, Aphrodite spoke once more. "Now, we must be off! Please step back so that I may summon transportation." After the crowd had backed away to give her space, Aphrodite glided on pink sandals to the bottom of the steps. There she pulled the swan cart from her bag with a flourish—as if she were a magician pulling a rabbit from a hat—and set it on the ground.

Her arms outstretched, she gracefully whirled around three times. This wasn't actually necessary, but it was fun. Besides, mortals always enjoyed it when immortals put on a show! Her golden hair and the hem of her sparkly white chiton swirled outward as she chanted the spell in her most dramatic voice:

"Feathered swans, wild at heart.

Spread your wings to fly my cart!"

As her cart grew ever larger and more magnificent, the onlookers gasped in awe. They'd probably be talking about this all over Greece by morning. Especially since the gossipy Pheme was watching!

When all was ready, the three mortal girls joined Aphrodite in her cart. She nodded to two servants.

They stepped forward, carrying several sacks full of rose petals, which they handed up to her. As the cart lifted from the ground, it looked like the whole city of Athens had come to see them off. She and the girls tossed the rose petals, which fluttered downward like fragrant pink and red snowflakes as their cart whisked them away into the wide blue sky.

Below, the crowd went wild at the spectacle. Athenians, young and old, shouted their best wishes. "Good luck, Aphrodite!" some called. "Beat that Isis!" yelled others. A boy punched his fist in the air. "Greeks rule!" he shouted.

Swiftly, Zephyr and Boreas—the west and north winds—carried them southeastward toward their destination, the island of Cyprus. The Greek girls sat on the scalloped bench seats on either side of the cart and began asking Aphrodite questions.

"What's he like—this mortal boy we're going to meet?" Tessa asked.

"His name is Pygmalion. Pyg for short," Aphrodite told them.

"A nickname? How cute!" cooed Chloe, clapping her hands.

"I'm so-o-o excited!" said Zoe, bouncing on her seat and making the cart swerve.

"Me, too. Just think—if he picks me, I'll be famous all over Greece!" said Tessa.

"I think I'll faint if he picks me," said Chloe, falling over in her seat, pretending to do just that.

And some people claimed *she* was a diva, thought Aphrodite. She couldn't help smiling at their antics though. They were all so boy-crazy that they probably wouldn't even notice that Pyg was annoying and self-centered. Not one of them had asked what would happen if he did pick them. Would their friendship be long-distance, or would the girl and her family move to Cyprus, or would Pyg move to Athens? Well, her job was only to bring them together. The rest they'd have to figure out on their own later.

"What does Pygmalion look like?" Tessa asked, twirling a lock of her bright red hair around her finger.

"He's an artist," Aphrodite said, "with brown hair and chocolate brown eyes."

"Like a deer?" asked Chloe, her own gray eyes widening.

"Or a basset hound?" asked Zoe, as she popped a stick of pine gum in her mouth.

"Yes, I suppose so," said Aphrodite. "Sort of like either of those."

"Ooh." Tessa sighed. "He sounds adorable."

"Oh, he is," said Aphrodite, rolling her eyes. Pyg was not her idea of a good crush. She only hoped he was *their* idea of one! You just never knew, when it came to matters of the heart. She'd chosen carefully. These mortal girls all had much in common with Pyg. However, in the end, whether he liked them or they liked him would be up to them.

A few hours later, the cart touched down on Cyprus, and Aphrodite ushered the girls out. Minutes later, she was ringing the bell on Pygmalion's door with all three candidates standing right behind her, eagerly awaiting their first glimpse of him.

When Pyg opened up, her eyes fell on a small pink box with a glittery bow that he held in his hands. Noticing her studying the gift, he looked a little embarrassed, but didn't explain.

Had he wrapped this gift for one of the girls,

hoping to find true love among them? How sweet! Aphrodite softened toward him and sent him a smile.

Behind her, the girls giggled with excitement, drawing Pyg's attention. He frowned at them before glancing at Aphrodite again. "Who are they?" he asked in a loud whisper.

Aphrodite stepped aside. "Girls, this is Pygmalion, the mortal boy I was telling you about. Gesturing toward each girl in turn, she said, "Pyg, I'd like to present Tessa, Chloe, and Zoe." He stared at them blankly.

"They're the candidates I chose for you," Aphrodite reminded him, her brows rising. "In the matchmaking competition between Isis and me. Remember?"

"Oh, yeah." Pygmalion turned and studied the girls intently for about five seconds. Maybe less. Tessa giggled nervously, Chloe chewed on a fingernail, and Zoe tapped her foot impatiently. Then Pyg pointed at them, one after the other, and spoke decisively. "No. Nuh-uh. And absolutely not."

Aphrodite's mouth dropped open in surprise "What? But you didn't even give them a chance."

The girls, who were accustomed to being treated politely by the boys they knew, gasped at this insult, turning as pink as the gift he still held. And it certainly didn't look like he was going to give that present to any of them after all!

"How picky!" said Tessa, frowning at him.

"How icky!" said Chloe, folding her arms.

"How absolutely rude!" Zoe huffed.

Aphrodite completely agreed. So she didn't try to stop them when all three turned and stomped back down the path toward the cart. "I'll join you in a few!" she called after them. Then she put her hands on her hips and glared at Pyg. "What is wrong with you?" she demanded in outrage. "I interviewed hundreds of girls to find those three. They were perfect for you!"

Pygmalion sniffed. "They were *not* perfect."

"I didn't say they were *perfect*. I said they were perfect for *you*."

"In what way?" he challenged.

"They're all artists, for one thing. Tessa is a sculptor who has won prizes in the annual Art-o-thon. Chloe has been invited to sculpt a small frieze for Zeus's new temple in Olympia. And Zoe's work with marble busts was in last month's *Artmopolitan Scrollazine*. Besides that, they're dying to find a crush. And they like jokes." *Even lame ones*, she thought, but didn't say. "And if you had talked with them you might have found that out!"

"I didn't need to talk to them," Pyg said, seeming surprised that she disagreed with his rejection. "I could see they were all wrong right away. The first one had a weird giggle. I can't have giggles like that breaking my concentration when I'm working. The second one reminded me of someone who broke one of my sculptures back in second grade. And the third one. Don't get me started on what was wrong with her. Did you see how annoyed she got? I need someone with a sweet disposition, who'll give me peace in which to create. Someone who admires me and my work. Someone who understands that my feelings are delicate and easily crushed." He clutched his hands to his heart. "I'm an artist!"

Aphrodite gritted her teeth. "And you think that's an excuse for acting like a jerk?"

"A jerk? Me?" He looked down at his gift box, turning it over and over in his hands. Then he glanced up at her. "I didn't mean to hurt anyone's feelings, honest.

It's just that you know love when you feel it, you know? And they simply weren't . . . right. I only wish they had been." He heaved a deep, sad sigh.

Seeing his genuine disappointment, she calmed. A true goddess of love would try to counsel her client in this situation. So she said, "Sometimes love grows, if you give it a chance."

"Yes, I know," he said, surprisingly earnest. He shifted from one foot to the other, and she felt he was going to add something more—something important. "As a matter of fact, there's something I should tell you—"

Suddenly, they both heard footsteps coming up the path. She glanced around and saw Isis heading their way. And when Aphrodite looked back at Pyg, his expression had closed down like a door slammed shut.

"It's her turn now," he told her, dismissively.

"Very well." Confused and feeling let down,

Aphrodite didn't try to argue and only moved up the path toward the cart. What a disaster!

"How did you do?" Isis asked anxiously as they passed.

Aphrodite forced a smile. "Fine." But, of course, she hadn't done well at all! The three girls Isis had in tow were almost as exotic and beautiful as Isis herself, Aphrodite noted with growing nervousness. *What if Isis wins this competition?* she worried. *Then what will I have left?* She'd only be the goddessgirl of *beauty.* Of course, she was proud of that title. But the four Egyptian goddessgirls were all beautiful too. If they won the title of goddess of love away from her, would they then feel emboldened to challenge her for the title of goddess of beauty as well?

Back in Athens, everyone would be awaiting news of what had happened. They were going to be mad that

Pyg hadn't chosen a Greek girl. If he chose an Egyptian one, that was going to make them even madder. And then what would happen? Was her failure here going to start another war, uh, incident?

Behind her, she heard Pyg being his same old cluelessly bad-mannered self. She peeked back at him just in time to see him judge Isis's candidates as harshly as he had her own. Pointing to each of the three Egyptian mortals in turn, he announced his feelings loud and clear. "Nope. No way. And forget it."

Next thing she knew, the Egyptian mortal girls were storming past her, with Isis bringing up the rear.

"Some matchmakers you are!" Pyg shouted at them from his doorway. Aphrodite noticed that he was still holding the pink gift box. *Who in the world would he deem worthy enough to give it to?* she wondered. "So you're not going to choose either of us for the title of goddessgirl of love?" she called back to him.

He sighed deeply. "Well, I suppose I *could* give you each one more chance," he said at last. He acted like he'd be granting them a huge favor to do so.

Isis glanced at Aphrodite. "Do we even want another chance?"

"I'm not sure," Aphrodite whispered back.

Then Pyg called out again. "I'll grant you two more days. Come back the day after tomorrow if you think you can do better. Otherwise the whole world will soon know that *neither* of you deserve the title of goddess of love!" He slammed the door.

Aphrodite's hands clenched into fists. She pressed them to either side of her head. "Grrrr," she said. "If Pyg causes me to tear out my hair, that's just one more thing I'm going to be annoyed at him about!"

"I hear you on that, goddessgirl!" Isis agreed

angrily. They fell into step together, moving down the path along the bluff toward the cart. "Did he say the same thing to your girls that he did to mine?" Isis asked.

"Pretty much," Aphrodite admitted.

Looking relieved, Isis shook her head in annoyance. "I swear, if that Pyg says, 'I'm an artist' one more time . . . !"

Aphrodite laughed. "I know! Being an artist is no excuse for his behavior!"

"Who do you think that pink gift box was for?" Isis asked, darting a curious glance her way. "A thank-you gift for whichever one of us succeeded? Or was it meant for the girl he chose?"

"Hard to say," said Aphrodite. Isis's companionable irritation was making her feel less bad about everything. "It's weird the way he really seems to want to find love, but then won't give any girl a chance." Just then, she noticed Hermes' delivery chariot zipping by on its rounds overhead, and she waved him lower.

"Maybe we'll figure it all out tomorrow," said Isis, sounding tired. "You're going to try again too, right?"

"Unless you give up?" Aphrodite glanced at her in question.

Isis shook her head. "I can't. All of Egypt is rooting for me."

Aphrodite sighed as they reached the cart. "Same here with Greece." Since Ra's sunboat had already departed, and she needed to pick up her friends in Cairo anyway, she offered Isis and her girls a ride back to Egypt, after first sending the three Greek girls back with Hermes.

Isis spent the whole trip trying to soothe her mortal girls' ruffled feathers. They were understandably angry about Pyg's attitude. And a worrisome thought of her own kept Aphrodite occupied the entire trip too: What would the Greek girls tell everyone back in Athens?

Athena, Persephone, and Artemis waved to her as she approached the bazaar, their travel cases by their sides. "We saw you coming!" Persephone called as the cart drifted closer to the ground.

"How did it go?" Athena asked as the Egyptian girls piled out of the cart.

"Don't ask," said Aphrodite. With a quick, somewhat awkward good-bye to Isis, Aphrodite loaded her friends and their bags into the cart. Then they all headed north toward MOA. On the way home, the four goddessgirls shared all that had happened while they'd been apart. Aphrodite told her friends about the competition and what Pyg had said and done. But she still held back from telling them why winning the competition mattered so much, about her D, and her extra credit deal with Mr. Cyclops. In turn, her friends told her about the pyramids and how Hathor had tricked them so that they couldn't return to Greece in time to help her.

Aphrodite was disappointed to hear about Hathor's trickery. Had Isis been in on it? Surely not. Even though she and Isis were in competition, sometimes it seemed that they were becoming friends.

But as they neared MOA, her thoughts began to focus on other troubles. Up ahead, dark gray storm clouds hung low and thick over the entire school. Zeus was obviously still in a bad mood. A mood that was even worse than before, judging by those clouds! Had he heard what had happened with Pyg?

9

Boom! Zap! Crash!

As they flew closer to MOA, they heard a fierce thunderclap.

"Sounds like Zeus is still grumpy," said Artemis, covering her ears.

Then a flash of lightning zigzagged across the sky. "Looks like it too," said Athena. She sounded as concerned as Aphrodite felt.

"I wonder why?" said Persephone. "He's been acting even gloomier than Hades did when we first met."

They all watched the storm, silent for a few moments. Her friends looked so worried that Aphrodite's guilt for her part in all this grew. She was just about to confess that her mess-up in Hero-ology had likely caused Zeus's anger, when she noticed the tears in Athena's eyes.

"What's wrong?" she asked, touching her arm.

"Are you crying?" Persephone asked her in surprise.

"No," said Athena, turning her head away and blinking. "The wind blew something in my eyes. That's all."

The other three goddessgirls looked at one another other, certain she wasn't telling the truth. Something was really wrong!

"You've seemed sad for a while now," Aphrodite said, trying to coax her to talk.

"Yeah," added Artemis.

"Can't you tell us what's bothering you?" Persephone asked.

After a few seconds, Athena turned toward them, her face pink. She'd bottled up some kind of emotion and now she looked ready to explode with it. Finally words burst from her in a rush, "If you must know—my mom has left my dad!"

Aphrodite was shocked. "Metis left Zeus?"

"You mean, *left*-left? As in forever?" asked Artemis.

Athena nodded and then let out a sob.

"Oh, Athena, I'm so sorry," Persephone said, gently rubbing her back. "What happened?"

"What happened is . . . well, you know how my mom is a fly?" Athena said. They all nodded. "A few weeks ago, she said she just got tired of living inside my dad's head. So she buzzed off to be with her other fly friends.

She said only they could understand what it's like to have compound eyes and sticky feet."

Athena brushed away tears, but they kept flowing. Persephone reached into her travel case for a tissue. Athena blew her nose, then shrugged. "Mom and Dad never did get along all that well, but I never thought this would happen!" She let out another sob, and the other goddessgirls wrapped her in a group hug.

Quickly, Aphrodite murmured instructions to the swans so that the cart began to circle MOA instead of landing during the storm. It wasn't easy, but she refrained from asking all the questions she was dying to ask, sensing that Athena just needed to talk.

"Since my mom left, she's come back to visit twice," Athena told them between sniffles. "But it's just not the same as when she was in dad's head. She's too buzzy—I mean busy—with her new life. That's all she can talk about."

"Well, this explains why Zeus has been in such a bad mood," said Persephone.

"Yeah, and it looks like his mood is growing even worse," said Artemis, "Look!" She pointed toward the school courtyard below.

The girls looked over the sides of the cart. Red-faced and shaking his fists, Zeus was yelling at Mr. Cyclops. "Watch where you're going, you big one-eyed lummox!" he roared, as rain dripped from them both. "You almost mowed me down just now!" Students stared from the school windows, watching the whole thing.

"Oh, no," Athena moaned.

Aphrodite took Athena's hand and gave it a quick squeeze. "Sometimes unhappiness makes people lash out at others. Zeus is probably just lonely since your mom left him."

Athena's tears stopped as she stared at her in surprise. "I've been so sad and embarrassed over this that I've only been thinking about my own feelings," she said slowly. "But you're right. I guess he must be lonely. I mean, one minute my mom is talking nonstop inside his head, and the next—silence."

Persephone nodded thoughtfully. "It'll probably take some time for him to get used to it."

Down below, Zeus stomped off and the storm went with him. As it moved away, the last of its wild gushing winds unsettled the cart. It was all Aphrodite could do to steady it. "Hang on!" she told them as she took them lower. "This storm is passing, but there are new thunderbolt holes all over the place down there."

It was a bumpy landing and the cart skidded sideways across the rain-slick marble tiles of the courtyard. They came to a jolting halt only when the cart banged against a giant thunderbolt stuck in the tile. Overhead the skies were already turning light gray, then blue as the storm blew over.

"Good thing my dad went for another walk," said Athena.

"Just in time," Artemis agreed.

As the others grabbed their bags and left the cart, taking the steps up to the Academy's front doors, Aphrodite stashed the shrunken cart in her handbag, and then joined them. When they opened the bronze doors, they were astonished to see Artemis's dogs running up and down the halls. And Mr. Cyclops was there, yelling at Hades, "Get these mutts out of here!"

When their teacher noticed them, his eye narrowed. "Artemis! Get over here, young lady!"

Sensing she was in trouble, Artemis hunched her shoulders. "Uh-oh."

"I'll come with you," said Persephone, sounding worried. The two girls trudged toward Mr. Cyclops with the air of prisoners condemned to execution. Meanwhile, Hades tried unsuccessfully to catch the dogs. After two days of separation they were so happy to see Artemis that they became even giddier, bounding back and forth across the hall.

Suez jumped up and put his paws on Mr. Cyclops's back, almost knocking him over. As he caught his balance, he glared at Artemis and Hades in turn and yelled, "If someone doesn't get these dogs under control, I'll have them thrown out of MOA!"

"Suez, Amby, Nectar—come!" Artemis shouted, chasing after them. But they were too excited to obey. Amby grabbed Persephone's travel case with his teeth. Before she could stop him, he ripped the side of it open and pulled her clothes out. Then he and Nectar began tossing them in the air with playful jerks of their heads, as if it were all a game. Suez circled them, wagging his tail and barking.

Anger was as contagious as the flu, and it looked like Mr. Cyclops had caught Zeus's anger and was passing it on to Artemis, who was now yelling at her dogs.

Aphrodite wasn't sure anymore how much of the blame for Zeus's bad mood should fall on her, but surely some of it was her fault. After all, she'd started the ball rolling with the Trojan incident that had made mortals so mad.

Suddenly, Athena grabbed her arm, pulling her toward the stairs. "Can we talk for a minute?" she asked urgently.

Aphrodite went with her, still watching the wild scene before them. There wasn't much they could do here anyway, and Athena obviously needed to talk.

"Let's go up to my room," Aphrodite suggested. She practically had to shout to make herself heard over all the yelling and barking.

"Mine's closer. We can talk there if Pandora's out," Athena told her once they reached their hall. Not waiting for Aphrodite's reply, she peeked into her room. Since it was empty, they went in.

Athena tossed her bag onto her desktop and sat on her bed beside it. Almost immediately words poured out of her. "I want to talk to you about my mom and dad."

Aphrodite shut the door, then sat on Pandora's bed opposite Athena's. "Are you sure you wouldn't rather wait for Persephone if you're looking for advice? I don't have any experience with parents."

"But you do know about love," said Athena, leaning forward eagerly. "And I'm hoping you can help my dad."

Aphrodite's brows rose. "Me? Help Zeus?" The idea that the King of the Gods and Ruler of the Heavens could ever require anyone's help was a new and strange one.

"Yes. I think you're right about him being lonely. And since you have a Lonely Hearts Club, I'm wondering if you know someone my dad might like to hang out with." Athena paused for a moment. "You know, like a companion—a goddess his own age. Someone who doesn't mind his moods and . . . and the occasional thunderbolt hole."

"You want me to find someone to mend Principal Zeus's broken heart?" asked Aphrodite. *Yikes*, she thought. This was not a job she wanted. Everyone at MOA was a little afraid of the principal, including her.

"Exactly. So will you do it?" Athena asked.

"Well . . . ," Aphrodite began. Athena was obviously

rocked by her parents' split. Who wouldn't be? Still, the idea of putting herself directly in Zeus's path—especially now—was just plain frightening. What if he started taking his bad mood out on her? What if he decided to smite her or threw her out of school for interfering?

Athena reached to a shelf behind her and picked up the toy horse she'd brought with her from home when she'd first come to MOA earlier in the year. The very one she'd used as a Trojan horse in the Hero-ology game. "You know what the worst thing is?" she asked, hugging the toy to her chest and resting her chin on its mane.

"What?"

"When my mom was in Zeus's head I used to pretend that she looked like a regular goddess instead of a fly. But when she buzzed out of his ear and I saw she was a real fly, I was so disappointed. And I feel bad about that. I mean, she can't help it."

"And you can't help your feelings, either," Aphrodite said gently.

"So will you help me? Help my dad?"

Though she was inwardly shuddering at the notion, Aphrodite nodded. Athena needed her and she would not let her down. Though she still wanted to win the contest and improve her grade, those things weren't as important as helping her friend. "Okay. But first, I've got to get something. Wait for me." Dashing down the hall to her room, she picked up a copy of her matchmaking quiz. Hurrying back to Athena's room, she handed it to her. "It's a quiz," she explained. "To help me find a match for your dad. I need you to get him to fill it out."

"Let me see it." Since Athena's bag was on her desk, she unrolled the quiz on Pandora's desk, glancing over the questions. Then, she looked at Aphrodite.

"How am I supposed to get him to answer these questions?" she asked. "It's not like I can just tell him to. He doesn't like anyone telling him what to do."

"Tuck the quiz into one of those *Temple Digest* scrollazines he's always reading in his office," Aphrodite suggested. "No one can resist a quiz. Once he sees it, he's bound to take it, even if he's in a bad mood."

Athena brightened. "I know what you mean. I always answer those quizzes in *Teen Scrollazine*. It's like they're hypnotizing me: *You will fill me ouuut.*" As she let go of the quizscroll, it magically rolled itself up.

Beneath it, Pandora's desk was covered with homework. Aphrodite couldn't help noticing the cartoon doodles she'd made on the edges of her notescrolls. One was of two linked hearts, with a *P* in each. *P*s for Pandora and Poseidon, no doubt.

"Well, I'd better get going and let you unpack," said Aphrodite, suddenly remembering all the things she had to do. She still hoped to match Pyg, and she didn't want to let down Pandora, either. And she'd help Medusa, because in her heart she knew it was the right thing to do. But that didn't mean she had to like her. Plus, now she had to match Zeus. And that could turn out to be a full-time job in itself!

Athena jumped up, looking excited. "I'm going to sneak into Dad's office now, while he's gone, and slip this inside one of his scrollazines. Thanks." She gave Aphrodite a quick hug, then they both went their separate ways.

On her way back to her room, Aphrodite hummed a popular love song written by Apollo's band. Athena looked a lot perkier now that they had the beginnings of a plan to help her dad. The new challenge had lifted her own spirits too. Medusa was right. Even when things were in a mess, she could always find something that made her happy!

Back in her room, she remembered to check her mailbox. At first she thought it was empty, but then she felt the buzz of magic brush her fingertips. She'd gotten a letterscroll from an immortal. This one read:

YOU HAVE WOUNDED MY HEART

WITH EROS'S DART.

~ FROM GUESS WHO LIKES YOU?

Godness! A second riddlescroll? She did not have time for this on top of everything else. She was going to find out who had sent it. Right now! Stomping downstairs, she sought out Hephaestus. When she found him, he was working in his forge. Aglaia, the girl Aphrodite had encouraged him to hang out with, was helping him.

"See, you hold it in the fire with the tongs, then pull it out to cool," he was saying.

Aglaia laughed. "This is fun!" As she turned the tongs, Aphrodite noticed that a bracelet sparkled on her wrist. When Hephaestus had tried to get Aphrodite to wear it, she remembered suggesting that he give it to someone special. And it seemed he had. The pair looked like they were getting along just fine.

But she wanted to be sure. So before either of them noticed her, Aphrodite hid behind a cabinet of ironworking tools. Then she summoned a bird, and sent it fluttering to rest upon Aglaia's shoulder with a message asking her to meet one of her friends in the cafeteria. When Aglaia left, Aphrodite came out from her hiding place and joined Hephaestus.

His face lit up when he saw her. "Aphrodite! What brings you here? Need another golden apple for a race?" She smiled, shaking her head, knowing he was referring to the golden apples he'd once forged for her so she could help a mortal named Hippomenes find love.

Hephaestus was one of the nicest godboys she knew, but he was only a friend. She hoped he thought the same way about her. "No, this time I was wondering if you could help me with something that's not about metalworking."

"Sure, anything," he said, still working his tongs in the fire. "What is it?"

"Well, I'm writing a poem and I need a word that rhymes with 'sad,'" she told him. "Any suggestions?"

He tilted his head, his eyes going upward as he thought hard. Then he looked at her again. "'Unhappy'?"

he suggested. "Oh, wait, that's a synonym, not a rhyme. Well, how about 'cat' or 'gab'?"

"Hmm. Good options," she said, smiling at him again. He was superb at metalworking, but he obviously couldn't handle rhyme. Definitely not the riddle-sender. "Well, gotta run. Thanks again!"

As she left the forge, she tapped her chin with one end of the riddlescroll, thinking. If Hephaestus hadn't written those rhyming notes, who had? She eyed various godboys she passed as she crossed the courtyard, considering each of them in turn. They all perked up when they saw her looking their way. Could one of them have sent the note? There were just too many possibilities!

She sighed. There were other more important things to worry about right now besides who was sending her riddles. While she awaited Zeus's quizscroll answers, she needed to get to work on Pygmalion's situation. And then there was the Pandora-Medusa-Poseidon love triangle. She only hoped that didn't turn out as disastrously as the King Menelaus-Paris-Helen love triangle she'd foolishly created in Hero-ology!

As for Pyg—this time, she wasn't going to take actual girls to visit him. That hadn't worked out before, so now she would try something different. She'd take sketches of the new girls. Quickly, she shape-shifted into a lovebird and flew down to Athens. After returning to her true goddessgirl form again, she visited three other girls she'd interviewed the day before in the agora.

Now that she had a better idea of what Pyg did *not* want in a girlfriend, she hoped to make better choices. She wouldn't select girls who were sculptors or painters this time since he didn't seem to care if they were artists themselves. She'd only pick those who appreciated creativity—and seemed likely to be able to put up with a perfectionistic artist like him!

She informed each girl she visited that she'd been selected as a candidate for Pyg after all. Luckily, her new choices were enthusiastic to be in the second round. Then she asked each one to write a brief poem about herself, encouraging her to add humor and emotion.

After that, she went to the shop of a skillful artist and commissioned him to visit the homes of those three girls and create faithful likenesses of them on sheets of papyrus. She would return for both the likenesses and the girls' poems the next morning.

By the time she got back to MOA, Aphrodite was starving. And no wonder. She hadn't had any lunch and it was late afternoon by now! On her way to the cafeteria, she ran into Athena, who was holding a slightly scorched and rumpled quizscroll.

"Is that what I think it is?" Aphrodite asked, knowing it had to be Zeus's quiz.

Athena nodded, following her as she went to get a tray of food. "I tucked it into the latest edition of *Temple Digest* as you suggested, and it must have caught his interest because . . . voila! Here it is, all filled in."

"Hey!" called a voice. The two girls glanced up to see Persephone and Artemis entering the cafeteria. "We came for a snack," said Artemis, her dogs trailing her. "Grab our table, and we'll join you in a few."

As the two other girls finished filling their trays, Aphrodite whispered to Athena, "Should I put this quiz away for now, or—"

"No, it's okay for them to know," said Athena. "Maybe they can help."

"Help with what?" asked Artemis, setting her snacks on the table as she joined them.

"What's that?" Persephone asked, gesturing to the partly burned quizscroll with her spoon as she sat too. Then she dipped it into her ambrosia sundae and took a bite. "Yum."

Quickly, Athena and Aphrodite explained everything. Then all four girls leaned in, eager to examine Zeus's quiz.

"His handwriting looks like chicken scratches," said Aphrodite, squinting at it.

Persephone frowned. "I can't read it either."

"Don't look at me," said Artemis, shaking her head at it.

"I'll read it," said Athena, picking it up. "I have a knack for deciphering his writing. And besides, I'm not eating and you are."

Aphrodite took a sip of her nectar. "Okay, I'll say the questions—since I know them by heart. Then

210

you read his answers. First question is: 'What kind of animals do you like?'"

"And my dad wrote: 'All kinds,'" said Athena.

"Good answer," said Artemis, as she plopped three blobs of ambrosia on the floor by her chair. Her dogs quickly slurped them up.

Aphrodite went on, "Next question: 'What do you love most about yourself?' Let me guess," she added. "I'll bet he checked all the boxes for that one." She took a spoonful of soup.

"You got it," said Athena. "Apparently, he has a good personality, is smart, a good friend, handsome, creative, and he can keep a secret. Oh, and by 'Other' he wrote: 'Everything. What's not to like?'"

"Ye gods!" said Artemis. Making a noise that was half giggle and half snort, she pushed away her drink and quickly slapped a hand over her face. "That almost sent nectar out my nose." Which of course made them all laugh.

"Next quiz question," Aphrodite continued once their laughter died away. 'How would your friends describe you?'"

"I think we can all guess that answer without even looking," said Athena. The girls looked at one another and giggled. Then together they recited: "'King of the Gods and Ruler of the Heavens.'"

Athena checked to see if they'd been right. "Yup," she said. "And guess what his answer was for: 'What makes you a good catch?'"

The girls looked at one another again, and all together they took a wild guess: "'Mortals admire and fear me, and quake when I walk past.'"

"Right again," said Athena, laughing with them, for

these words were printed under Zeus's portrait in his office. Aphrodite's heart lifted, seeing her friend look so much happier than she had been lately.

Athena continued, "Next up is: 'How would you describe your ideal companion?'"

"Now, this is a very important one," said Aphrodite. She leaned toward Athena, listening intently.

"It's a long answer," said Athena, taking a deep breath. "'A woman who is smart, strong-willed, and has skills and interests of her own. Someone I can talk to and who doesn't giggle too much or mind scorch marks. Someone who doesn't have compound eyes or sticky feet or give me a headache.'"

"Interesting," said Aphrodite. "Now we're getting somewhere." At least Zeus knew what he was looking for in a companion. Pyg only seemed to know what he *didn't* want. Setting her empty bowl aside, she thought for a minute. Then she stood up. "Come on, grab some winged sandals and let's get going."

"Where?" asked Persephone.

"To the Immortal Marketplace," Aphrodite replied.

"Ugh, I hate shopping," Artemis complained.

"Don't worry. It's not the kind of shopping you're thinking of," Aphrodite assured her as the girls left the cafeteria and grabbed magic sandals from the basket beside the school's front door. "We're going to the Marketplace to shop on behalf of Athena's dad. 'Cause I have a feeling it's where we might find exactly who he's looking for."

10

Hera

WITH THEIR MAGIC SILVER-WINGED SANDALS on, the goddessgirls skimmed across the courtyard at ten times their normal walking speed. Minutes later, they gently touched down in front of the enormous, glass-ceilinged Immortal Marketplace. Quickly loosening the straps at their ankles, they looped them around the wings to hold them in place so they could walk normally. Then they waited a few minutes for Artemis's dogs to catch up. The hounds were fast runners, but keeping up with winged sandals was impossible even for them! Luckily, dogs were allowed in the Marketplace—as long as they behaved themselves.

Once inside, Aphrodite pulled Athena along past dozens of shops separated by rows of tall Corinthian columns. Persephone, Artemis, and the dogs followed in their wake.

"This is crazy," said Athena, looking around. "I know they sell almost everything here, but you can't go shopping for a *wife*!"

Artemis's jaw dropped. "Is that what we're doing?"

Aphrodite grinned. "No, not a wife exactly. We don't even know if Zeus will want to wed again. It's probably much too soon for that. For now he needs a companion. A friend. A lady to hang out with. He's used to having Metis around, so he's lonely for the sound of a feminine voice."

"You're probably right. But what makes you think we'll find someone for him here?" said Athena.

Aphrodite gestured from one end of the mall to the other. "This place is full of immortal women. Where else could we go and find so many in one spot?"

Persephone nudged Athena. "How about that one?" she asked, pointing with her chin toward a pretty goddess with a shopping bag over her arm. Her makeup was perfect and she wore her hair in a complicated hairstyle of waves and curls.

"She looks sophisticated enough for Zeus all right," Athena mused.

Aphrodite nodded. "Artemis, why don't you send your dogs in her direction, so we can see how she reacts to animals."

"Good idea," said Artemis. She bent over and whispered a command to them, and suddenly all three bounded off. When the goddess saw them coming, she let out a sharp squeak, shied away, and then ran into a store to get away from them. Artemis whistled, and the dogs came trotting back, all innocence.

"Not an animal lover, I'm guessing," said Athena, shaking her head.

"And did you see how she ran away?" said Aphrodite.

Persephone nodded. "Much too fearful for Zeus."

"Yeah, he'd squash her like a bug," said Artemis, rubbing her fist in the palm of her other hand to demonstrate.

Persephone elbowed her sharply, shaking her head.

"Ow!" complained Artemis. "Why'd you do that?" Then she must have remembered that Athena's mom was in fact a bug, because suddenly she looked contrite. "Oh, sorry, Athena."

Athena smiled slightly. "It's okay. I know you didn't mean anything by it."

Suddenly, Aphrodite squealed. "Ooh! Look!"

The others turned in the direction she was pointing, searching for another possible love match for Zeus. But there weren't any women passing by right then. "Where?" asked Athena.

"There." Aphrodite dashed over to stand before a store-window display that featured a bright blue chiton. "Look! Isn't it dreamy? It's the exact color of my eyes. It's almost like it was made for me. C'mon. Let's go in."

Artemis laughed. "I thought we were supposed to be shopping for a friend for Zeus, not a chiton!"

"Hera's Happy Endings," said Persephone, reading the sign above the door. "Hold up a minute." But

Aphrodite had already gone inside. The others trailed after her, a little uncertain.

Inside, the store was stuffed with froufrou dresses in every color of the rainbow. There were long gloves and shoes dyed to match, as well as tiaras and books with ideas for invitations and flower arrangements.

"I think this is a wedding shop," Persephone whispered as they stood huddled together just inside the door.

Aphrodite's shoulders slumped a little as she realized they were right. "Oh, I guess that means the blue chiton is a bridesmaid's dress. Never mind, then." She needed to focus on what they'd really come to find, anyway.

"Let's go," Athena said, nudging her. "Customers come here only if they're already engaged to marry. We won't find a woman for my dad in here."

Just then a regal-looking shop-goddess came toward them. She had thick blond hair styled high upon her head and a no-nonsense look in her eye. Although she wasn't unusually tall, something about her made her seem statuesque.

"*Au contraire*," said Aphrodite, perking up. "I think this may be just the place to find what we're looking for." She peered at the shop-goddess's name tag. It read: HERA.

"Young ladies!" the goddess greeted them in a firm voice. "We have expensive, delicate fashions in here. Dogs aren't allowed."

"You don't like dogs?" asked Artemis.

Hera smiled. "I didn't say that." She gave each of Artemis's dogs a pat. "However, lacy wedding gowns and dogs do not mix. Take them outside the shop, please. And here, you may give them these." Going to the shop counter, she reached into a jar and pulled out three dog treats.

Artemis grinned. "Thanks." As she walked past the other girls to take her dogs out she gave them a thumbs-up. In case they hadn't guessed what she meant, she whispered the words: "I like her. For Zeus, I mean."

"Do you own this store?" Athena guessed, since the goddess's name was the same as the shop's name.

"I do," Hera began. Then, hearing a customer arguing with one of the other two shopkeepers, she murmured, "Excuse me," and went to take care of the matter.

The goddessgirls watched her calm the annoyed customer. "She obviously has interests and skills of her own," said Persephone. "I haven't heard her giggle, either."

"And since she's a good businesswoman," added Athena, "she must be smart."

"I wonder how she feels about scorch marks?" mused Aphrodite.

Just then, Hera returned. "Now what can I help you with?"

The girls stared at her blankly. Finally Athena blurted, "How do you feel about scorch marks?" Then she put a hand to her mouth, looking embarrassed.

"We're looking for a wedding gift," Aphrodite quickly improvised to cover Athena's blunder. "For her dad."

"You're Zeus's daughter, aren't you?" Hera asked Athena. "I thought you looked familiar."

"You know my dad?"

Hera laughed, a hearty melodious sound. "No, but I know of him. Who doesn't? I've always admired your father. But he's married to Metis. Why does he need a wedding gift?" She tilted her head to one side.

"Or perhaps I've misunderstood. Are you his personal shoppers? Is he going to be *attending* a wedding?"

The girls looked at one another, trying to come up with an answer.

"You're not really shopping for a gift, are you?" the sharp-eyed Hera guessed.

"You're right." Aphrodite elbowed Athena. "She is smart," she murmured.

"Yes, and I have excellent hearing," said Hera.

Aphrodite blushed.

"The truth is that my dad's not married anymore," Athena admitted quietly. "My mom left a few weeks ago."

"Oh, honey, I'm sorry to hear that," said Hera kindly, putting a gentle hand on her shoulder.

Aphrodite and Persephone met each other's gaze over Athena's head. Persephone's expression seemed to echo what Aphrodite had already decided. This woman would be good for Zeus—and for Athena.

Thinking quickly, Aphrodite said, "We were wondering if you could come to our Hero Week dance this weekend at MOA. We need a chaperone."

"Oh!" Hera said in surprise. "Well, I suppose I could. The store closes at night." She paused. "Should I bring anything? How about a cake? If there's one thing I know about besides fancy dresses, invitations, and flowers, it's cake."

Moments later all was arranged, and the four goddessgirls were retracing their way through the marketplace again, about to head back to school. Hanging out with her friends had been fun, but Aphrodite's heart sank a little now that it was time to focus on her Pyg problem again. She wondered how Isis was doing in her second search for suitable girls.

Now that she was getting to know her, Aphrodite felt kind of bad that one of them had to lose the contest in the end. In other circumstances, she had a feeling they could have been friends. Still, she was determined to win. Not only to prove herself, but for the good of MOA and the Greeks!

When they passed Cleo's Cosmetics, Aphrodite glanced in the window, then stopped at the sight of Cleo, the purple-haired, three-eyed makeup lady behind the counter. As long as she was matchmaking, she might as well go all out!

"You guys go on. I'll catch up." Without waiting for a reply, she dashed into the store, spoke to Cleo, and caught up with her friends again minutes later.

"What did you do?" Artemis asked.

"I talked Cleo into coming up to MOA to do makeup for all the girls before the dance. Besides being fun, I told her it'll help advertise her store," said Aphrodite.

"Cool!" said Athena.

Aphrodite smiled. After she'd given Athena a makeover earlier that year, Athena was taking more interest in such things.

"Isn't Cleo the lady you once said would be a good match for Mr. Cyclops?" Persephone asked, interrupting her thoughts.

Aphrodite grinned. "Maybe."

"You're matchmaking again, aren't you?" said Artemis.

Aphrodite laughed. "And why not? If Mr. Cyclops hits it off with her, I figure it could only help his bad mood too, right?"

And maybe it would help her grade, as well!

11

Galatea

HELLO? APHRODITE CALLED OUT, AS SHE rang Pygmalion's doorbell the following afternoon. It was the second time she'd rung, and still no answer.

Earlier that morning, her swan cart had taken her from Mount Olympus Academy to Athens. There, she'd picked up the papyrus sketches of the three Greek mortal girls as well as the poems they'd created overnight. Now she was on the island of Cyprus once more, standing on Pyg's porch holding the six scrolls—three under each arm.

She was just about to ring him a third time, when she heard a noise coming from behind his house. Curious, she walked around to his backyard and found him standing beside a table, arranging a bouquet of freshly picked flowers rested in a lovely vase. As he carefully stuck a rose between two violets, he mumbled something. Going still, she paused to listen.

"Roses are red.

Violets are blue.

Flowers are sweet.

And you are too."

It was a love poem, Aphrodite realized in surprise. Could it be that this strange boy actually had a tender side? His poem seemed to indicate that he might truly be looking for love and hoping she—or Isis—would find him someone he could give his flowers to. His loneliness touched her heart.

"Pygmalion?" she said softly.

"Oh!" He let out a squeak and jumped in alarm. "You again!"

She nodded. "Those are beautiful," she said, stepping closer to examine the flowers.

Before she could get anywhere near them, he snatched the vase up and clutched it to his chest. "What do you want?" he asked.

"We had an appointment, remember? The match-making competition?" she prompted.

"Yeah, I remember," he said unenthusiastically. "Come on inside, then."

Honestly, did this mortal want to find love or not? Confounded by his attitude, Aphrodite followed him through a side door into his house and down the hall. Once they reached his art studio, he said, "Wait here." Then he disappeared behind an enormous linen curtain he'd hung from the ceiling to hide the back portion of his studio. It hadn't been there on her last visit, Aphrodite remembered. When he came back out, he no longer had the flowers. However, the bouquet's fragrance still hung in the air. And she smelled something else too. A *mystery*. There was something he didn't want her to see behind that curtain. Why was he being so secretive?

Pyg came toward her. "So where are the new candidates?" he asked, as if he'd just noticed that she hadn't brought anyone with her.

"This time, I decided to bring the likenesses of mortal girls to show you and poems they've written as a way of introducing themselves." She set the bundles of scrolls she'd been carrying on the closest table, pushing aside some art supplies. Then she unrolled the first three scrolls, one at a time, displaying the likenesses of the girls. As he gazed at them, Aphrodite read aloud the poems each girl had written. When she finished, she had to brush away a tear. The poems had all been lovely—full of humor and emotion just as she'd requested.

"So what do you think?" she asked him brightly. He'd probably like all three, but she'd come prepared to guide him in narrowing his selection to one. "Aren't they wonderful?"

Pygmalion sighed. Pointing to each likeness in turn, he told her, "Uh, no, no, and no."

She gasped, wanting to throttle him. "But what's wrong with them?"

To her surprise, Pyg dropped his head. "I—I don't

really know," he mumbled, staring down at the floor.

"Well, if you don't know, then how can you just reject them so quickly?!" Aphrodite exclaimed in exasperation.

Lifting his head again, he shot her a look filled with anguish. "I don't know how to explain this. I know you're trying to help me. But I have a confession to make. You see, for a long time I've had this idea about the perfect girl stuck in my head, and—"

Ding-a-ling! Just then they heard someone ring the doorbell on the far side of the house. Aphrodite's breath caught. Isis, no doubt.

"I'll be right back," Pyg told her. He glanced toward the linen curtain, then gave her a wary look. "Don't touch my stuff, okay?"

"Uh-huh," she sort-of promised, folding her arms. But the minute he left, she slipped behind the curtain to snoop.

Back here, the fragrance of Pyg's flowers was strong. Glancing around, she saw the vase at the base of a statue that was covered with a long drape. It was the same one he'd stopped her from viewing on her first visit. Curious, she walked over to the statue, which was about as tall as she was.

She reached out to peek under the drape, then recalled her half-promise not to touch anything. Still, for a goddess, snooping while keeping such a promise was easy. Whirling a perfectly manicured, pink-polished fingertip in the air, she created a gentle breeze that lifted the drape higher and higher.

From the bottom up, a statue chiseled from the finest gleaming white marble revealed itself, inch by inch. First, only the hem of the sculpture's flowing skirt was visible, then a belted waist, two slender arms, shoulders, and long wavy hair. Soon, Aphrodite was staring into the face of one of the most flawless and beautiful girls she'd ever beheld. Pyg might be a lot of annoying things, but he was also an incredibly gifted sculptor.

But why had he set his flowers here? Beside them sat a cage with a small lovebird inside. The minute the drape had lifted, it had begun to sing its high, clear notes. She put a finger to her lips, shushing it. Immediately, the bird quieted. Then she noticed something else. Behind it sat the bright pink gift box from yesterday!

She straightened, excitement flooding her. The flowers. The lovebird. The pink box. These were all tokens of affection. Gifts. Was Pygmalion in love with the girl who'd modeled for this sculpture? Of course! That would explain why he'd rejected all the other girls. His heart was already taken! Why, then, had he sent Isis and her on a wild goose chase to find him a new crush? Did this girl already have a crush? Was he too bashful in her presence to tell her of his affection? Or what?

As she stood gazing upon the statue, she heard Pyg return to the studio with Isis. Quickly, she slipped outside the curtain and stood in the shadows at the back of the studio to watch. Her stomach did flip-flops as she worried her competitor would best her. Then she realized Isis had no chance of winning this competition either. Pyg's heart was already taken.

The moment Isis began her presentation, Aphrodite was reminded how much they really did think alike. For Isis, too, had brought sketches of her candidates this time, instead of actual girls. Instead of poems, however, her girls had written songs. Same difference, though.

Once again, Pyg rejected them all. "But any of these girls would be perfect for you," Isis insisted. "Why are you rejecting them? Is it because you prefer one of the girls Aphrodite presented?"

"No, that's not it at all," Aphrodite replied. Stepping from the shadows, she went to stand beside the curtain. "It's because he is already crushing on someone else." And with that, she shoved back the curtain to reveal the statue. "Her!" she announced dramatically.

With a look of alarm, Pyg leaped past her. "What have you done to my beloved?" Running to the statue, he circled it worriedly, examining it for injuries.

"Don't worry, I didn't touch her," Aphrodite assured him. "I've only been admiring her. She's truly stunning."

Isis joined them at the rear of the studio, "Who is she?" she asked, obviously awed by the figure's beauty.

"Her name is Galatea," Pyg admitted. "And you're

right. She is my crush. My supercrush. My mega-crush." He clasped his hands over his heart as he gazed upon the statue.

"But she doesn't return your affections?" Aphrodite guessed.

He nodded sadly. "When I heard about the Lonely Hearts Club, I wrote my letter, hoping the goddess of love could find someone as perfect for me as Galatea is." He sighed. "But I should have known that was impossible. Just as my crush on Galatea is—impossible."

He looked so downcast that Aphrodite's anger at being sent on a wild-goose chase evaporated. When it came to love, mortals sometimes did dumb things. Immortals, too.

"Maybe we could speak to her on your behalf," suggested Aphrodite.

"We?" Isis asked, glancing at her.

The "we" had slipped out by accident, but now Aphrodite was glad it had. She genuinely liked Isis, and she was sure Isis liked her, too. She smiled. "I think it's time we worked *with* each other instead of *against* each other," she said. "What do you say?"

A slow smile spread on Isis's face. "I say you're right. So what do you say, Pyg? Would you like us to talk to her?"

Pygmalion shrugged, looking hopeless. Then he gestured to the statue. "Be my guest."

"Well, I don't think she meant we'd talk to the statue itself," said Aphrodite. "What good would that do? But if you tell us where we can find this Galatea—"

"You're looking at her," Pyg interrupted.

Aphrodite and Isis stared at each other, brows raised in confusion.

"You mean you're in love with the actual *statue*, not

239

the girl who modeled for it?" Aphrodite asked him in disbelief.

"What model?" Pyg asked, sounding puzzled. "I never use models. The ideas in my head are so much better."

So that's why he'd told them to go away when he'd thought they were models that first day they'd come here! Aphrodite realized.

Going down on one knee, Pyg gazed at Galatea with adoring eyes.

"Aw, that's so cute," Isis murmured, obviously touched.

"Poor Pyg," said Aphrodite. "You truly do love her, don't you?"

"How could I *not* love Galatea?" Pyg gushed. "She is my masterpiece. Every day as I sculpt here in the studio, her eyes tirelessly admire my work. When I tell her my jokes, her smile makes my heart sing with joy.

She is everything to me. " His voice turned sad. "Alas, her heart is made of stone." Hunching his shoulders, he stood and trudged away.

"I never thought I'd ever say this in a mummillion years," said Isis, watching him sink down on a chair at the front of the studio. "But I actually feel sorry for him. I only wish there was something we could do."

Aphrodite nodded, thinking hard. Suddenly an idea came to her. "Maybe there is."

Isis glanced at her.

"There's this girl at my school," Aphrodite explained. "A mortal named Medusa. She once turned Athena's roommate, Pandora, into stone. But then Athena used a de-stone spell to change her back."

"And you think that same spell might work in this instance?" Isis asked, sounding enthusiastic as she caught on.

"It's worth a try," said Aphrodite, her own excitement rising. Not wanting Isis to think that the spells of Olympic gods were boring, she decided to spice up her magic so it looked more impressive. Scooping up handfuls of flowers from the vase, she murmured to them as she tossed them high. Her magic caused them to spin around and drift down in slow motion. Some chained together to form a necklace around the statue, and others settled in its hair or floated lower to decorate the pedestal.

As they continued to rain slowly downward, Aphrodite stepped close to the statue and placed a hand on its cold, white wrist. In a dramatic voice, she cast her spell: *"Flesh and bone—return from stone!"* Then she released the statue's wrist and leaped back, ducking to avoid being hit by flying marble chips when the statue transformed.

Only there were no flying chips because nothing happened.

"Hmm," said Aphrodite, straightening. "I'm certain that was the right spell. I wonder what went wrong?"

"Maybe you need to adjust it a little," suggested Isis. "After all, that girl Pandora started as flesh, right? Then she turned to stone and back to flesh. But Galatea is starting as stone. So she might require an altered spell." She grinned. "Though I did like the flashy magic show."

"Thanks." Aphrodite grinned back. That Isis had seen through her attempt to spice things up wasn't really that surprising since they were alike in so many ways. "And you're right, of course. I'll try tweaking the spell." She thought for a minute, then stepped close to the statue once more. Tossing a heap of flowers high again, she sent some of them dancing in the air in wide swoopy rings that encircled her and the statue. Then she touched Galatea's delicate wrist while chanting new magic words: *"You started as stone—now become flesh and bone!"*

Aphrodite leaped back, breaking through the flower rings, which then drifted to the floor. Both girls waited, eyes glued to the statue, their hopes high. After a few seconds, the statue began to shudder. Marble cracked. Chips popped from it. A fine powdery dust filled the air as stone slowly transformed into skin, hair, chiton, and delicate sandals. Moments later, Galatea, now a mortal girl, blinked at them with violet-colored eyes. "Where's my beloved?" Looking beyond them she called out, "Pygmalion?"

At the sound of her voice, Pyg raised his head and glanced over his shoulder. Tears of joy filled his eyes as he beheld the girl of his dreams, now wholly flesh and blood. Springing up from his chair, he ran to

Galatea and knelt among the flowers scattered at her feet. The pair gazed at each other, and the mutual adoration in their eyes was plain to see.

"Oh, this is so romantic," whispered Isis, leaning close to Aphrodite.

"I know. Isn't it amazing?" Aphrodite whispered back. "I *love* happy endings!"

Pygmalion opened his lips to speak to Galatea. The two goddessgirls breathlessly awaited his declaration of love. But instead, these were his first-ever words to his beloved: "What did the block of marble say to the chisel?"

The two goddessgirls snorted in disbelief, but Galatea just tilted her head, thinking. "I don't know. What?" she asked after a few seconds.

"You crack me up!" Pygmalion replied, and the two of them laughed uproariously.

Isis and Aphrodite looked at each other. "His first words to her are a dumb sculptor's joke?" Isis whispered.

"To each their own," Aphrodite whispered back. "At least Galatea laughed."

As if he'd just remembered that the goddessgirls were still there, Pygmalion turned to face them. "Which of you accomplished this miraculous act?"

"Aphrodite," Isis admitted.

Pyg went to his worktable and found some papyrus and a feather pen. "Then I shall write an announcement and have it spread across the land, that Aphrodite is the one and only true goddess of love!"

Aphrodite almost let him do it. She almost did. She had wanted that title all to herself more than anything. But now that it was finally within reach, she found that having it all to herself again didn't matter as much as she thought it would. Though Isis was smiling bravely, as if losing the goddess of love title didn't really matter to her, Aphrodite knew it was an act. Just like Isis had known that Aphrodite's dramatic tossing around of the flowers was only an act. She put herself in Isis's sandals, imagining her despair. The Egyptian goddessgirl hadn't tried to claim any credit for helping Pyg find love. And she did deserve some.

"Not so fast!" Aphrodite heard herself say. Pyg shot her a questioning look, his pen poised above the papyrus. "Isis fixed my spell," Aphrodite said. She felt the Egyptian goddess glance at her in surprise as she went on. "Without her help, it wouldn't have worked."

"I see," said Pyg, twirling the pen between his fingers, "So the title should go to—"

"Both of us," Aphrodite said decisively. "It was a tie. You can write two announcements—one that proclaims me to be the goddess of love and one that

247

proclaims Isis to be. We'll share the title." Which was pretty much the way things were before, when they didn't even know about each other.

Isis's startled green eyes stared into her blue ones. "Are you doing this because you feel sorry for me?" she asked.

"Not at all," Aphrodite said firmly. "It's only fair that you get half the credit." In truth, she could hardly believe what she'd just done either. But deep down, it felt right.

Sharing the title of goddess of love wouldn't take anything away from her own power at all. In fact, it might actually be nice to have someone she could occasionally confide in long distance—someone who understood the ins and outs of love as well as she did.

With copies of Pyg's proclamations in hand, the two goddessgirls said goodbye to him and Galatea, and took their leave. The two mortals were already making plans to build a cottage for Galatea nearby overlooking the rock quarry, and Pyg promised to introduce her around the village so she could make some friends.

As they headed down the path to the cart, Aphrodite sighed, feeling a contentment that had been missing for days. "Looks like Pyg and Galatea are set to live happily ever after," she said. "He's still clueless and his jokes are terrible. But Galatea seems to think he's a natural-born comedian and all-around awesome guy."

Isis laughed. "So they'll probably get along great."

Aphrodite grinned. "Good thing. 'Cause I have a feeling she is the one and only girl in the world who could appreciate him!"

Getting serious, Isis said, "Thanks for what you did back there. If you had kept the title all to yourself, no one would have blamed you, not even me."

"*I* would've blamed me," said Aphrodite. "It wouldn't have been fair. I couldn't do that to a friend."

"Friend?" Isis's eyes lit up.

Aphrodite smiled. "Yes, *friend.*" She gave Isis a hug. Suddenly she had an idea. "Could you come to MOA instead of heading back to Egypt right away?" Aphrodite asked her. "There's a dance tonight, and a makeup expert from Cleo's Cosmetics is coming to give makeovers. I have an extra bed in my room. You can sleep over and I'll take you home tomorrow. What do you say?"

"I say yes!" said Isis. She held up her hand and the girls high-fived. *High fives must be a universal language too, like pinky swears,* Aphrodite thought.

When word got around down on earth that she and Isis had hung out at the dance together, everyone would know that they were buds. And that would erase any chance of a war between Greek and Egyptian mortals who had sided with one or the other of them. Inviting Isis to the dance was a friendly thing to do, but it was also smart thinking. Whoever said beauty and brains couldn't go together was wrong, Aphrodite thought. She had both!

12

Guess Who!

Aphrodite's dorm room served as "central makeover headquarters" that night before the Hero Dance began at MOA. Cleo from Cleo's Cosmetics had come as promised to give makeup advice to the two dozen goddessgirls who dropped by. All three of her eyes lit up every time a new girl came in for a makeover. Inspired by Isis's exotic look, Aphrodite,

Athena, Persephone, and Artemis asked to have their eyes lined with kohl. When others saw them, they began asking for the same look. Isis smiled, obviously flattered.

The girls had all dressed in costumes representing their Hero-ology heroes. Athena was wearing a boat headdress because her hero, Odysseus, was currently sailing homeward. Since Paris was prince of Troy, Aphrodite was dressed in a princely fashion, wearing a toga woven of purple velvet and a small silver crown in her long golden hair. She wore sparkly silver stockings and sandals, and had powdered her face and hair with silver glitter to match.

As Aphrodite and Isis watched Cleo work, the three of them discussed techniques such as proper eyeliner application. They could have talked makeup tips all night. But there was a dance to get to.

"C'mon, we're running late," called Persephone as

the sky darkened outside. Her crush, Hades, was busy in the Underworld that night, but she wasn't one of those girls who couldn't have fun without a godboy to flirt with and was as excited as everyone else about the party. "I can already hear the band warming up over in the gymnasium!" she said. Though it was some distance away—the classrooms and dorms were separated from the gym by sports fields—the sound of Dionysus on his double-reeded aulos and Apollo plucking at his seven-stringed kithara carried faintly. Soon Persephone and the others headed off.

Aphrodite and Isis were the last ones to go out the door. Just as they were leaving, a magic breeze whooshed in through Aphrodite's window. "Hold on a sec," she said to Isis." Hurrying to her mailbox, she pulled out the small papyrus scroll that had just come in. Magic buzzed her fingertips.

"A letter?" Isis asked.

Aphrodite nodded. Opening it as she headed out of her room, she saw that it was another riddlescroll. Her *third*!

"What does it say?" Isis asked, seeing her puzzled expression. As they walked outside and across the school courtyard, Aphrodite read it aloud:

I WAS ON YOUR SIDE IN THE TROJAN WAR.

WHEN I THINK OF YOU, I THINK: "AMOUR."

~ FROM GUESS WHO LIKES YOU?

"Ooh! Someone is mashing on you," said Isis, sounding excited.

"Huh?" asked Aphrodite.

"Isn't that what you and Pygmalion were saying earlier to mean when someone likes you?"

Aphrodite laughed with sudden understanding. "You mean crushing. Someone's crushing on me."

Isis looked a little bewildered. "Either way, it is mysterious, yes?"

"Definitely," agreed Aphrodite.

Which of her many admirers could have sent it? Everyone at MOA took Hero-ology, and students had been evenly divided between both sides of the Trojan conflict.

She tucked the riddlescroll in her pocket as she and Isis arrived at the dance just behind the other goddessgirls. The gym had been decorated to resemble the Hero-ology game, with bright murals on the walls depicting different countries, cities, and beasts, as well as Greek heroes and their glorious feats. Colorful banners hung around the room and torches had been lit here and there. The bleachers had been pushed back and tables heaped with food lined the far wall.

Up ahead, Artemis waved to her brother Apollo on the stage with his bandmates, Dionysus, Ares, and Poseidon. Artemis had helped him write the song they were playing now, a popular tune called "Goddessgirls Just Wanna Have Fun." Apollo waved Artemis up, and she joined them onstage, harmonizing with him.

Aphrodite and Persephone pulled Isis onto the dance floor, so she would feel like part of the group. The girls drew a lot of attention when Isis began showing them a new dance called "Walk like an Egyptian." With their bodies facing forward, they turned their heads, feet, and hands, so that their noses, toes, and fingers pointed toward one side. Moving their arms and legs to the beat of the song, they took a few steps in one direction, then turned and went the other way. More and more immortals joined in until the whole dance floor was doing it.

Spying Hera mingling with some of the other teachers off to one side of the room, Aphrodite looked around for Zeus, who always came to chaperone the dances. He wasn't here, though. She certainly hoped Hera didn't leave before he arrived!

Seeing Medusa standing off in a corner with her sisters, Aphrodite sighed. Medusa's arms were folded and she wore a scowl. Honestly! Some people had no idea how to have fun. Since her hero was a king, Medusa wore a gold crown. Unfortunately, her snakes had decided to curl up and nap in the middle of it. It looked like she was baking a green snake casserole on top of her head!

Naturally, no godboy went near her. Yet, Aphrodite had a feeling Medusa didn't realize just how odd and unfriendly she looked. She probably just figured boys didn't talk to her because they didn't like her. Of course, her reptile hair didn't help. Still, Aphrodite's belief that there was someone for everyone hadn't changed.

If anything, her experience with Pygmalion had made that belief stronger! And she actually had a godboy in mind for Medusa. Not the one the snaky girl liked. She didn't think Poseidon was right for her. Instead, since opposites sometimes attracted, she'd selected a godboy who was the complete opposite of Medusa. A boy who lived to have fun—Dionysus.

As soon as he and Ares climbed down from the stage for a break, leaving the rest of the band to continue with songs that didn't require them, Aphrodite seized her chance and headed for the unsuspecting fun-loving boy. A few steps from her goal, she bumped into Ares. Literally.

"Whoa!" he said, grabbing her arm to keep her from falling and then gently setting her back on her feet. "I was hoping I'd run into you here, but not quite like that!" He gave her a dazzling smile.

Aphrodite stood on tiptoe, looking past him for Dionysus so as not to lose track of him in the crowd.

"Could I talk to you for a minute?" Ares asked.

Her attention caught, Aphrodite looked up into his sparkly blue eyes and felt herself blush. Ares was the only godboy at MOA who had that effect on her. Often she wished that he didn't, since most of the time she was mad at him about one thing or another. Although she'd never admit it, arguing with him was kind of fun. "Sorry, now's not a good time. There's something I need to do."

Ares' eyes darkened slightly. "Later, then, okay? I—"

But Aphrodite was barely listening now. Dionysus was heading for the door! "Yoo-hoo!" she called out, dashing after him. When she caught up to him, he looked at her in surprise. "What's up?" he asked.

"Um," she said, trying to figure out how to get him to ask Medusa to dance. Then she noticed the bandana peeking out of the pocket of his toga. "Is that the blindfold you wore at the agora the other day?" she asked.

Grinning, he whipped it out. "The one that says 'love is blind'?" he asked, displaying it.

"Yes!" She laughed lightly. "That was so funny. You should wear it here."

"You think?" His eyes, which were the color of purple grapes, brightened. He was always ready to try something fun, unlike Medusa. Quickly he wrapped the bandana around his head, tying it at the back.

"Oh! I see a girl waving at you already," she told him. "Here, let me take you to her. No peeking now." Aphrodite took his hand and led him to Medusa, who was still standing like a statue in the exact same spot she'd been in before. "Dionysus wants to dance."

Looking stunned, Medusa looked left, then right. Seeing no one else around, she pointed to herself. "You mean with me?"

Aphrodite nodded. Narrowing her eyes, Medusa whispered, "Why is he wearing that blindfold?"

Hearing her, Dionysus laughed. But fortunately he didn't seem to recognize her voice. He pointed to the saying on the bandana. "Because love is blind. Get it?"

"It's a game," Aphrodite explained. "He's going to try to guess who you are after two dances. Don't give him any hints, though."

"Lead me to the dance floor, my lady." Dionysus crooked an arm toward Medusa. "Time's a-wasting. Only two songs to make you fall in love with me."

Medusa giggled. Actually giggled! Well, maybe it sounded more like a cackle, but still. Aphrodite couldn't recall her ever having cracked a smile that wasn't mean before. As the pair headed for the dance floor, a slow song began. Aphrodite tensed when Medusa's snakes hissed, as if they were humming to the tune.

Dionysus's expression turned puzzled. "Are there some balloons leaking somewhere?" he asked. She couldn't hear Medusa's reply, but Aphrodite sighed with relief. Crisis averted. The pair seemed to be off to a good start, chatting away. She only hoped that the "love is blind" slogan would hold true when Dionysus finally saw who he was dancing with.

"Matchmaking again?" asked a male voice.

She turned to see Ares at her side. "Maybe."

He shook his head in amusement. "But Dionysus and Medusa? That's a strange combination."

She sent him a superior smile. "I know what I'm doing. I can sense romantic sparks before they even fly." He was standing so close to her that their shoulders and the backs of their hands were touching. Her cheeks began to feel warm.

Ares snorted a laugh and murmured, "Yet you don't notice when someone likes *you*."

Aphrodite's heart gave a flutter. But then she remembered the current thing she was mad at him about. Turning toward him, she poked a polished purple fingertip in the middle of his chest. "What I told you about my grade the other day at the agora was private. You should have known that. I didn't appreciate you telling your friends. I haven't even told my own friends yet!"

Ares eyes widened innocently. "I didn't tell them!"

She stared at him, suddenly uncertain. "But right after I told you, you said something to your friends, then they looked straight at me and laughed!"

"They weren't laughing at *you*," he said. He ran his fingers through his thick blond hair, looking frustrated, and a little embarrassed. "They—"

Ares' eyes flicked to something beyond her and Aphrodite turned to see Isis approaching. Her beautiful green eyes were glued to him. And who could blame her? Ares was the cutest boy in school, no question.

Aphrodite fought to squash down a spurt of jealousy. After all, she and Ares were history, right? After she made the introductions, there was an awkward pause. To fill it, she gestured toward the dance floor. "Why don't you show Ares that new dance, Isis?" she suggested.

Immediately she wanted to kick herself. What was

she doing, putting the two of them together? Ares was bound to be drawn to Isis's exotic beauty. She wasn't sure why she cared, but she did. Behind her back she crossed her fingers, hoping Ares would make an excuse for why he couldn't dance right then.

Instead, he just gave Aphrodite a strange look. There was something in his eyes she couldn't quite interpret. *Disappointment?* But then he favored Isis with a polite smile and gestured to the dance floor. "All right, let's hit that floor, goddessgirl!" As the pair moved away, Aphrodite couldn't help thinking how beautiful the two looked together. But not wanting to think about Isis's hand on Ares' arm, she tore her eyes away.

Just then Poseidon hopped down from the stage to take a break, and she remembered she had another romance to kindle. Casually, she fell into step beside him. While complimenting him on how well he played the lyre, she herded him toward Pandora, who had cornered another godboy and was peppering him with questions.

"Oh, hi, Pandora," she said when they drew level with the girl. When Pandora turned toward them, the boy she'd been questioning saw his chance and dashed away from her interrogation in relief. Too bad the curious girl didn't seem to know how to hold a normal conversation.

Yet, as soon as Poseidon greeted her, the usually gabby Pandora became completely tongue-tied. Poseidon fell silent too.

Aphrodite rolled her eyes. Godness, what would mortals and immortals do without her? she sometimes wondered. They'd never fall in like, much less in love, that was for sure. Catching Pandora's eye, she nodded toward Poseidon, who was studying the prongs of his trident. *Ask him about himself,* she mouthed silently.

"What?" Pandora asked loudly, leaning closer to her.

Poseidon glanced at them as if he'd overheard. When his eyes rested on Pandora, his glittery cheeks flushed. This was a surprise even to Aphrodite, for half the girls in school had crushed on Poseidon at one time or another and he'd rarely seemed affected.

"Nothing," said Aphrodite. But when Poseidon looked away again, she whispered to Pandora, "Ask him one question."

"About what?" Pandora asked.

"About himself. Maybe about his . . . um, his trident. And then listen to his entire answer before you say another word."

Pandora looked thoughtful, then nodded. Stepping closer to Poseidon, she asked, "So what's the difference between a pitchfork and a trident anyway?" Then she pressed her lips together like she was trying her hardest to hold back another question.

Poseidon's face lit up instantly. This was a topic that was near and dear to his heart. As he began to explain, Aphrodite quietly slipped away. When Apollo and Artemis began a duet with a catchy beat a few minutes later, she was gratified to see Poseidon lead Pandora onto the dance floor.

Isis and Ares seemed to be having a good time dancing out there as well, Aphrodite couldn't help noticing. She forced her attention elsewhere, immediately spotting Mr. Cyclops. He was already talking to Cleo, the makeup lady! It appeared they'd found each other without her help. And they were making what Artemis sometimes called goo-goo eyes at each other.

Three romances down, one to go. And the last one was the most important. Right on cue, Zeus strolled into the gym, holding a big black umbrella and looking morose. His eyebrows were drawn together in a frown and his eyes roamed the room restlessly. With every step he took, thunder shook the floor. Shrieks of surprise sounded as it began to drizzle through the open-air roof and inside the room! All over the gym, umbrellas popped open. A black cloud hung over the party now, everyone's joy dampened. If she didn't do something fast, the dance would be ruined.

But before she could decide what to do, Hera walked over to Zeus, all confidence and determination. Aphrodite held her breath as Hera introduced herself and held out her hand to him. When he shook it, tiny sparks flew between their clasped fingers, but Hera didn't seem to notice. Zeus gazed at her as if bewitched. Then he invited her under his umbrella, and the two of them began to talk.

As Aphrodite stood watching, Athena, Persephone, and Artemis joined her under an enormous multi-colored umbrella that Artemis had found somewhere.

"I wonder what she's saying to him," Athena whispered.

"I don't know, but whatever it is seems to be improving his mood," said Persephone. She stuck her hand outside the umbrella. "The drizzle has stopped."

"Hey, you're right." Artemis snapped the big umbrella shut, shaking droplets from it.

Within minutes the black cloud over the room vanished, and custodians rushed to mop the floor. Soon the band struck up a new tune, and students moved onto the dance floor again. Meanwhile, Zeus and Hera continued chatting away, seemingly unaware of what was going on around them. Zeus was even smiling now, and laughing, too.

Gray eyes sparkling, Athena turned to Aphrodite and hugged her. "This is the happiest I've seen my dad in ages. Thank you!"

"Is it hard seeing him with someone new, though?" asked Aphrodite.

Athena shook her head. "If Dad likes Hera, that's enough for me. I just want him to be happy."

"So do we," Persephone and Artemis said at the same time. The goddessgirls laughed.

But then Athena's face fell and she grabbed Aphrodite's arm. "Ye gods! I think my dad just asked her to dance!"

"Oh no," said Aphrodite turning to look. Sure enough, Zeus and Hera were moving onto the dance floor. Though he didn't seem to realize it, Zeus was the worst dancer in the world. The four friends could only watch in horror as he began a jerky mix of the hula, the swim, and the twist. Persephone cringed. Artemis groaned. Athena's shoulders slumped. "This romance is doomed before it can even get started."

"Maybe not! Aphrodite said in excitement. "Look!" To the goddessgirls' surprise, Hera was still smiling. Was it possible she found Zeus's weird, uncoordinated dance somehow endearing?

"Aw, look how cute they are together," Persephone said.

"Goo-goo eyes," said Artemis, pretending to be disgusted.

But Athena had gone silent and was staring at the entrance to the gym. Aphrodite followed her gaze, and saw that Athena's friend Heracles had just entered. His eyes roved the crowd, searching. When they found Athena, he grinned and made a beeline for her. He didn't even seem to notice any of the other girls. Aphrodite liked that about him.

Moving away, Aphrodite looked for Isis. When she spotted her, she was dancing with a different boy. So where was—

Just then, the band struck up a new song—one she hadn't heard before. Ares moved to the front of the stage, and she realized that he was going to sing it.

"This is a song I wrote," he announced. "It's called 'Who Likes You?'" In a strong, steady, voice that seemed to fill the gym, he began to sing:

You've got the smarts

To help Lonely Hearts.

Guess whooo . . . likes you?

Aphrodite straightened, her eyes going wide. Wait a minute! That sounded very familiar. Could it be that the boy who'd once said he would never be caught dead sending flowers to a girl, had actually written a song for her? But it seemed it *was* true. For as the song continued, he sang all the lyrics from the riddlescrolls she'd gotten, one after the other. Ares was her mystery guy?

All over the gym, goddessgirls sighed and murmured, watching the handsome godboy onstage. When the song ended they cheered for him. Although he shot the crowd a smile, Ares didn't seem to notice all the adoring girls. Instead, he hopped from the stage and made his way straight to Aphrodite.

"So it was *you* who wrote me those riddlescrolls!" she said.

He nodded. "That's why those guys were laughing that day at the agora. They weren't laughing at you. They were teasing *me*. Because of the song. They knew I wrote it about you." He paused, tucking both hands in his pockets. "Did you like it?"

275

"What girl *wouldn't* like a song written about her?" she said. "But did you mean it?"

Ares looked her in the eye. "Every word." He hesitated. "Look, Aphrodite. I know I—"

"Stop." Aphrodite held up a hand to shush him. "The words of your song were so incredibly sweet. You might risk ruining it if you keep on talking."

Laughing happily, he took her hand and dropped a light kiss in the center of her palm. "You know me too well." She folded her fingers over the kiss, holding it tight. "Dance?" he murmured.

"Sure," she said dreamily. As he drew her onto the dance floor, the gym seemed ten times brighter and sparklier then it had a minute ago. Was it just that the dark clouds surrounding Zeus for so long had finally lifted? Or maybe it was simply being near a boy she liked. One who liked her back.

Nearby, Isis was dancing with yet another boy. She looked like she was having the time of her life. Aphrodite caught her eye and they sent each other little waves.

Then Mr. Cyclops happened by, twirling Cleo in his arms. Who'd have guessed he'd turn out to be such a good dancer with those big feet of his!

Aphrodite smiled at him over Ares' shoulder. Just that morning she'd slipped a full and honest report about all that had happened with Pygmalion onto his desk. "B?" she asked now, daring to hope. To her delight, Mr. Cyclops gave her a big thumbs-up.

Aphrodite beamed, her happiness complete. Wait till she told her friends what had really been going on over the holiday. In just five days, she'd turned her D for dumb into a B for brilliant, blissful, and beautiful!

Not bad for a sometime-diva. Not bad at all!

JOAN HOLUB is the award-winning author of more than one hundred and twenty-five books for young readers, including *Shampoodle, Knuckleheads, Groundhog Weather School, Why Do Dogs Bark?* and the Doll Hospital chapter book series. Of the four goddessgirls, she's probably most like Athena because she loves to think up new ideas for books. But she's very glad her dad was never the principal of her school! Visit her at joanholub.com.

SUZANNE WILLIAMS is the award-winning author of almost thirty books for children, including *Library Lil, Mommy Doesn't Know My Name, My Dog Never Says Please,* and the Princess Power and Fairy Blossoms series. Her husband says she's the Goddess of Annoying Questions. (Most having to do with why her computer misbehaves.) That makes her kind of like Pandora, except that Pandora never had to deal with computers. Like Persephone, she also loves flowers, but she doesn't have Persephone's green thumb. Suzanne lives in Renton, Washington. Visit her at suzanne-williams.com.